A Boon for
Baphomet

A fantasy cyberpunk novella

DeWitt Wilcox

Spiderpig Press
ATHENS, GEORGIA

A BOON FOR BAPHOMET

Copyright ©2017 by DeWitt Wilcox

All rights reserved. Published in the United States by Spiderpig Press, Athens, Georgia.

www.spiderpigpress.com

ISBN: 978-0-9989366-0-4 (trade paper edition)
ISBN: 978-0-9989366-1-1 (e-book)

Library of Congress Control Number: 2017941767

Printed in the United States of America
First United States Edition

Cover and Interior Design
K. Fletcher

Cover Photo Credits
Derived work from "Downtown Seattle from Kerry Park" by Tiffany Von Arnim, used under CC BY.

To the Brotherhood of the Duck,
whose support, friendship, and inspiration
made this story possible.

You are enablers
in the best of ways.

CONTENTS

Excerpt: Carter Sinterklas. "Bringing an English Tutor to a Gun Fight: Historicizing *himitsu no itaku.*" In *Inversions of Agency: Essays on Structural Power in the Immanentized World,* edited by Elena Orphanides, 67-89. Copenhagen: Weekly World Elsevier, 2061.

"THIS 'BROKERED SECRET AGENT' EMPLOYMENT model had become common among organized crime syndicates that took inspiration from the brutal efficiencies of the Japanese educational services industry, but it was not until the Labor Insurrection of 2018 that zaibatsu started to adapt the itaku model to facilitate industrial crime in the private sector (Nakano, 2025). Once foreign corporations witnessed the market advantages that itaku adoption had given their Japan-based rivals, the concept spread globally, not unlike a novel influenza mutation, as hypercapitalism devoured the political and cultural immune systems of established nation states. Privatized security and corporate law came to dominate these societies in the twenty-first century as neoliberal policies increasingly superseded and eroded their civil legal codes.

Itaku agents fill two roles in this broader, de-nationalized context. They solve tactical problems (particularly in the areas of human resources, media relations, logistics, and research and development acceleration) more cheaply and faster than lawyers for the megacorps. At the other end of the employer spectrum, they also provide smaller interests and individuals a more personalized alternative to a market-based legal system focused on its bottom line."

FRIDAY
14 DECEMBER, 2074

7 DAYS UNTIL WINTER SOLSTICE

CHAPTER 1

WHIT HAD A PUERQUITO HALFWAY to his mouth when the spirit manifested in front of his table at Cafe Jalisco. It stood over two meters tall with a lean build and hovered above the floor, amplifying its height. The radiant anthropomorphic figure had wings that reached in successively broader pairs from its ankles, back, and shoulders. In its left hand it carried a broadsword nearly as tall as itself, held point down. It raised its right hand, palm facing him, with the index and middle fingers pointing up, the other fingers folded under the thumb. The spirit appeared for less than a second in the material plane, but Whit could sense it waiting nearby in the astral.

He recognized it as Azcall, a spirit allied with a mage he knew and respected, albeit warily. Alcime Vannetais was one of a handful of mages west of the Mississippi who had a working knowledge of Enochian, in conversation with angelic spirits as well as versed in its theoretic applications. The others included a planar geographer who worked for Wayfarer in Denver, an elderly bachelor high priest who lived in Salt Lake City, and the head archivist of the arcane collections at the Huntington Library far to the south in Los Angeles. And, of course, there was Whit himself.

He glanced around the cafe. At eleven on a mid-December Friday morning, it was mostly empty in the lull between the morning rush and afternoon wave of University of Washington students. Finals week was wrapping up, too, and he'd finished his last appointment tutoring undergrads for the quarter. The few people still there were jacked into the matrix, taking advantage of the quiet and the free hardware acceleration. Whit's own allied spirit, M'pixl-tpff, had wandered off in search of new mortals to eavesdrop on. An inveterate social butterfly with the attention span of a fruit fly, they were not the Holy Guardian Angel that Whit had expected to receive after completing the Abramelin ordeal nearly three years ago, but in the intervening time he had accepted that they were probably the Holy Guardian Angel he deserved.

Whit sighed and put down the *pan dulce*. He slid his mind into the astral plane, where Azcall was waiting for him. He felt the ambient mana vibrate around the spirit's luminous crimson and gold form as they idly beat their six wings back and forth in the pale grey expanse. Ripples of translucent lavender energy swirled and disappeared in the turbulence they created.

Toatar. Zirdo zonrensg. The spirit's greeting vibrated through him as though he stood next to an immense bell. They spoke without moving their mouth, the polyphonies of their voice ringing slightly out of phase in Whit's astral ears like an out-of-tune carillon. *HARKEN, I AM DELIVERED TO YOU WITH A MESSAGE FROM MY MASTER, HE WHO WORKS WONDERS IN THE DEPTHS. PELE PIADPH. HE WHO IS KNOWN TO YOU.*

"I hear and acknowledge you," Whit replied in Enochian. "And your master. What's the message?"

AN UNSPEAKABLE MESSENGER WILL COME UNTO YOU ANON. GRANT IT AUDIENCE AND HEAR ITS PROPOSITION WITH FAVOR. The spirit paused before continuing, *THOUGH IT IS A WORK OF WEAK UNDERSTANDING AND INEPT CRAFT. ADPHAHT.*

"Did Alcime say that last bit, or was that all you?" he asked.

Azcall said nothing, but they grew slightly taller and arched their back.

"*ETHARZI.*" He raised a hand in acquiescence. "Doesn't matter. What sort of proposal is this, dare I ask?"

MY TASK IS FULFILLED. GEIAD LUCIFER. OUR LORD OF LIGHT. The spirit raised the sword in a salute and disappeared.

"*ZORGE* to you, too," Whit muttered as he pulled his mind back into the material plane. He took a bite out of the pig-shaped cookie and waited with resignation for the Ghost of Christmas Past to make its unspeakable entrance.

Fifteen minutes later, a black Song Motors sedan pulled up to the curb in front of the Neo-Mayan coffee shop. Whit watched in his peripheral vision as the driver got out. She opened the limousine's back door, and out hopped what appeared to be a small satyr. It wobbled on tiny hooves to the cafe entrance. After the satyr—a faun, really—nearly fell over trying to open the door, the driver darted in to rescue it. Whit looked at the odd pair astrally. *Ah.* The driver was human, with a weak aura that indicated significant cyberware implantations. The creature had no lifeforce aura of its own. In its void was a definite spirit form, though, but not a powerful one.

The faun wobbled over to Whit's table and climbed up onto the closest empty chair. Despite its lack of physical coordination and labored movement, it was eerily quiet. Whit realized the creature wasn't breathing. Up close, he could tell that the faun was an artificially constructed chimera. The bottom half had come from a goat, while the torso above the hips had come from a dwarf. Possessing a necromantic construct like that violated the SEAplex legal code in at least a dozen ways. To parade one around in public was unthinkably brazen, and he doubted whoever had made it was its current owner. The seams where the two halves joined were swollen and red, and the proportions were wrong. The deceased dwarf looked like he had been a young man when he died, but it had been a small goat, and the result was absurdly top-heavy. It smelled unnatural as well, the too-sweet trace of death undercutting barnyard musk and cedar, with a top note of hyacinth.

Whit could appreciate Azcall's disapprobation.

The faun settled in the chair and stared at him with milky eyes.

He stared back. "Have you come to take me away to Fezziwig's party?"

No response. Whit scanned the cafe and realized none of the other people were reacting to the creature's presence. He pulled a cigarette from the pack of Nat Sherman Naturals in his bag and lit it with a spell. Neither the owner stacking plates behind the counter nor any of the patrons took notice of his gross violation of social mores and public health codes. Whit wasn't sure whether they were under a spell, or if he and the faun were shielded from their awareness by an illusion.

He took a drag on the cigarette and blew a smoke ring in the air above him. He looked around the café for a response. Nothing. He glanced into the astral. A bubble now surrounded the creature and was just large enough to include him as well. The room outside its circumference appeared distorted, as though he were looking at shapes refracted through a glass of water. Using the faun's clumsy entrance to mask the nothing-here shield's spellcasting was nicely done, albeit gimmicky. His awareness slid back to the material plane, and he considered the faun that the unknown mage was using as a proxy.

"Useful, if creepy. Now what do—"

The faun opened its mouth in a wide gape, tilted its head back, and inhaled deeply. The mouth did not move as an uneven voice emanated from it, forming words without the aid of the bluish lips or blackened tongue.

"We are aware of your work, as a *himitsu no itaku* and agent of change in the shadows. We wish to hire you to right a wrong."

SUNDAY
16 DECEMBER, 2074

5 DAYS UNTIL WINTER SOLSTICE

Chapter 2

"SO, SOUNDS LIKE WE GOT another Johnson with an unnatural love of the dramz," Sakura 2000 said to him the the next day as she hacked the reserved parking space on a cross street at the east edge of downtown. The spiked bollards retracted into the pavement, and she backed her rally raid-spec, extra-long wheelbase Land Rover into the tight space.

Whit had met her two years ago, on his first job, when they were all pugging itaku gigs independently. They'd found themselves thrown together on a corporate extraction job with another mage, a spirit ranger, and a twitchy hacker, and to everyone's surprise they worked well as a team. No one got anyone else killed, the job got done, and they all got paid. They had continued their professional relationship as extralegal specialists for hire on over a dozen more gigs since then. The rest of their itaku team had messaged that they were on their way to the rendezvous point where they would regroup before heading to the Johnson appointment. The team's newest member called himself The Original Itaku, and had replaced their first hacker. He had begged off the evening's client meeting, however, and messaged that afternoon that he had other responsibilities to handle:

>**Sorry, chummers. Hate to let you down, but I can't make a meat node right now. Got some personal drek to defrag, but I can do some tac-pen and overwatch from the back 40.**

Sakura, the team's drone rigger, stepped out of the armored driver's compartment and shut the heavy door with a twirl of gathered skirt and lace crinoline. She slid her hands into the pockets of her princess coat, made from vid cloth that she'd programmed with a loop of fig leaves falling against a powder blue sky. She rocked back on the heels of her patent oxblood Mary Janes to look at the building across the street. "Was picking this place to meet supposed to be ironic or what?"

"You have no idea. It comes with the territory," Whit said as he opened the passenger door. "That was surprisingly subtle for this crowd."

She looked over her shoulder at him, her coat's high collar partially obscuring her features. "It's a little weird that you know them so well."

He made a pained face. "Not really. I wouldn't say I know any of them 'well,' but it's not weird that I know of them. You know what a small world it is for magic types in Seattle." He stepped down from the passenger compartment without bothering to check for oncoming traffic and walked around to the other side of the vehicle, where Sakura had moved to stand on the sidewalk.

She raised a doubting eyebrow at him.

Whit huffed. "Look, every town is a small town when it comes to its magical community. Well," he amended, "maybe not true for places like São Paulo, or Chengdu, obviously, but it's absolutely the case for Seattle."

"Okay. But you. You!" She leaned forward and poked him in the chest, the azure ringlets she had tied up into ponytails bouncing. "And Satanists. How does that even work?"

He swatted her finger away, nonplussed. "What do you mean? It's not like I hang out with them at Friday night potlucks."

She gave him a level stare. "Hello? Mr. Enochian Mage? Who talks to 'angels?' Although I don't get how Megapixel qualifies as one of those, but whatevs," she finished under her breath.

Whit gave a hapless shrug in return.

"Shouldn't you be, like, mortal enemies?"

He threw his head back and laughed. "Their mortal enemies are each other. The only time they aren't denouncing each other's sects is when they're busy jockeying for power within their own. I'm a neutral party as far as they're concerned."

"The God stuff doesn't bother them?"

"What God stuff?" He rummaged through the numerous pockets in his white oilskin parka for cigarettes.

"Okay, this's been bugging me." Sakura frowned as she watched him. "But do you, like, even go to church, Mr. I Have a Holy Guardian Angel?"

Whit remembered enduring the interminable Sunday services his childhood housekeeper had taken him to when his father was out of town and blanched at the prospect. "Why would you even ask that? Of course not! Although…" He looked away.

She smirked. "Yeah?"

He shook his head. "Nothing."

"Oh, come on! " She waved a hand in protest. "You do, don't you?"

"No! Oh, my God. I mean…" He doubled over with renewed laughter and then tried unsuccessfully to catch his breath. Maybe he should think about cutting back on the cigarettes. "Not literally my God, because that's, at best, a dangerously misguided notion that perpetuates oppressive dialectics, while eliding and obfuscating the obvious cosmic peril that sort of psychic container invites." He managed to get his breathing under control again. He stood back up, still clutching his sides.

Sakura sniffed. "I have no idea what that means, so I'm going to ignore it."

"Fair enough. However, to return to your original query: no, but—qualifier—we used to sneak out to events at the Cathedrale Fumanda on weekends when I was in boarding school. I still go to the pontifex's blessings here once in a while. Does that count?"

She shrugged. "Maybe? What kind of events?" She squinted as if a likely succession of lurid demimonde possibilities were flashing through her head. "Wait, 'pontifex?' You mean the Weed Pope?"

"His Holiness Scrog I? Yeah."

"Yeah." She shook her head. "Nope. Doesn't count."

"Oh, hey!" Whit pointed at a storefront at the end of the street. "There's a Grindcore. Mind if we stop there first? I could murder a Solstice Spice Latte."

"Enochian hipster," she muttered in resignation as she set the active security protocols on the Rover and followed him down the block.

The rest of the team was waiting for them in front of a shuttered commercial building a couple doors up and across from the meeting site, Eden. The iconic nightclub stood out among the glass high-rises and squat historical edifices that packed the downtown grid down the hill to the waterfront. The building dominated the street, with passivated ferrocrete walls sculpted to look like rough natural rock that tapered downward. Thick, fluffy clouds slowly drifted around its base, obscuring the lower floors and creating an overall effect of a floating island unmoored from its earthly bonds.

Bob Barker, DVM, had the collar of his stained duffle coat

turned up against the wind. Most of his face was buried under a thick scarf, but what little of the former veterinarian's face did show looked cross and uncomfortable. He was a surly mage in his late thirties who nurtured a hostility to the world so strong that it gave Whit mild nausea when he viewed the other man's aura astrally. Bob's self-sufficiency, boldness with magic, and sense of self-preservation benefited everyone on the team, however, and offset his personality deficits. Mostly.

Billy was standing next to Bob. The spirit ranger waved to Whit and Sakura with his usual good humor as they walked up and showed no sign of minding the chill, despite going shirtless under his deerskin vest. Whit wasn't sure if this was a result of his magical threshold training in wilderness survival or just Billy being, well, Billy. When he and Sakura had suggested the three of them form a magical lodge after their first year of working together, Whit readily agreed. He felt more at ease with them than with Bob, or even with most other mages, despite their not being fully magically active.

Whit looked up at the corner of the building and noticed the archer had neutralized the security cameras covering their position with a couple of well-aimed splat arrows. The location he had chosen for their rendezvous gave them a clear view of the infamous nightclub's entrance, whose cut-glass canopy glittered six stories above street level. The front door was staffed by a hulking troll who was playing an AR game on his comm HUD. He poked at the air in front of him, ignoring the line of hopefuls on the other side of the golden electroluminescent rope that separated them from the entry. On almost any night of the week, a long line of people would be there hoping to get in, but on a Sunday evening, the crowd was at ebb tide.

It was a slow night not only for the club in Seattle but also for its smaller, satellite locations connected virtually in real time across the world. It was early Monday afternoon in the Shibuya club, and the patrons jacked in there were mostly salarysuits meeting for lunch, uninterested in dancing or mingling. The Paris location was also empty at 06:00 GMT, the remaining people there passed out and too exhausted or intoxicated to make it home before the start of the work week. The only people outside on the elaborate wrought iron ramp that spiraled around the outside of the SEAplex location were a smattering of obvious tourists and a couple of middle-aged orcs at the front of the line. The latter were dressed incongruously, the woman in a pink pantsuit and the man in a long, black cloak. They were arguing with the bouncer at the rooftop door under the iron and glass dome.

Bob nodded to Whit and Sakura as he acknowledged their arrival. "I did some astral recon while we were waiting." He cleared his throat and looked pointedly at the synthcaf cup in Whit's hand. "I tracked several magically active people going into one of the warded rooms down below and pegged a couple of spirits hanging around them that aren't affected by Eden's wards. The more powerful one will be a handful if we have to fight. If these guys are who we're meeting, they came loaded for bear."

"So? We come loaded for bear," Billy said, unimpressed.

Bob circled his finger at the other itakus. "For the sake of argument, let's say we're loaded for black bears." He pointed to Eden. "Those guys? They're loaded for grizzlies."

"Ah," Billy said, mulling it over. He moved around them for a clearer line of sight to the nightclub entrance. He tilted his chin over his shoulder to talk to them but never took his eyes off the building across the street. "Are we the grizzlies?"

"They may be loaded for grizzlies," Whit said, "but I doubt we're the ones they're gunning for. They're probably hoping to impress the other big-game hunters in the room, so to speak."

"You wouldn't think a nightclub would be a safe place for bears," Billy said in a distracted voice.

Sakura hid her smile behind her hand and stifled a chuckle. "I think any bears can probably handle themselves."

Whit opened his mouth to say something, but after a pause closed it and decided to let the quip pass unvoiced.

"No bears to worry about here. Just some jackasses." Bob exhaled loudly and turned to Whit. "You were saying?"

"There's always a lot of posturing with this crowd. They love one-upping each other. Dominance spectacle comes with the territory," Whit said. He looked thoughtfully at the thick clouds circling the base of the building. Rumor said the club had bound a pair of elemental spirits—one of air, one of water—and compelled them magically to produce the meteorological effect. It was potentially dangerous, and arguably unethical, but over the long term it probably saved the club money compared to the cost of a comparable mechanical system. It definitely had more style.

"Normally there's nothing Satanists hate more than other Satanists. It's one of their greatest joys in life," he continued. He popped the lid off the cup of synthcaf and blew at the fragrant steam. "To see them set aside their sectarian differences like this… It's kind of heartwarming." He snickered. "I like to think of it as a Christmas miracle."

"Or suspicious," said Bob. The perpetual furrow between his brows deepened. His mouth twisted as he eyed the base of the building that hid the meeting space within. "Do you have any heads-up for us on who else we're meeting there? I thought we were dealing with your guy."

"He's not my—never mind." Whit frowned at the other mage and shook his head. "Alcime wasn't sure who would show at the meeting. He said the job was being underwritten by an ad hoc committee of local sects, most of which are at odds with the others in some way or another. They've agreed on Alcime as *vox corporum,* but they don't trust him or each other enough to delegate Johnson duties entirely."

"Oh, that sounds delightful," Bob crooned. He smiled mirthlessly. "Not the usual lone corporate asshole to double-cross us this time! We get a whole committee of crazy Johnsons at each other's throats, instead. That should work out great for us."

Whit crouched down and leaned back against the cold, concrete wall. He slipped out of his body and into full projection. A few of the nearby buildings had faint signatures that indicated low-level warding or barriers. He rose up through the astral twilight and saw the concentrated light of living auras shining across the street. The building that contained them appeared as a dim, barely perceptible shape, except for the vivid wards that marked its lower parts.

He moved closer to the club to check out what Bob had reported. A guardian spirit patrolled the space above, wary of his presence but not actively hostile. Below it were maybe a couple hundred living auras in the space that Eden occupied in the material plane. Most of them read as mundane, but here and there he saw auras that read as magically active as he slid frictionlessly through the space. The aura light from living vegetation, more muted and diffuse, traced the contours of interior rooms and blanketed the rooftop terrace. He reached the lower levels, where the meeting room was located. The astral barrier Bob had described blocked any auras within from sight, and the wards prevented him from coming closer. Two spirits hovered outside the barrier, however. They were not bound to the building, but nonetheless were barred from passing the warded perimeter, as he was. The less powerful one was a spirit of air that Whit didn't recognize, but sure enough the other one, the one that Bob had singled out as a potential threat, was Azcall. The spirit turned to him and gestured to the room with an elegant ripple of fiery wings.

Whit pulled back into his body and stood up, stretching his long limbs. "I don't think we'll get trouble from that spirit if we don't start any."

Bob snorted. "What, did you exchange friendship bracelets?"

"Friendship bracelets? Are we doing those, can I have one too?" asked Billy, turning his attention away from the nightclub entrance momentarily to grin at the two mages.

"No, I—" Whit glanced at him uncertainly before continuing. Billy had a deadpan sense of humor that could be hard to parse. Like when he claimed he had moved to the metroplex because "Grandma said it would be educational." From what Whit had pieced together over the past two years, "Grandma" turned out to be the eigengeist spirit who mentored Billy in the esoteric arts. Whit still hadn't figured out what educational value she though SEAplex itaku work could confer, but eigengeists were "free spirits" in more than one way and had their own agendas. "I recognized it. If there's some hostile power-play in action, I can't see it directed at us. I suspect whoever's behind this has a more subtle goal than a violent showdown in the city's most fashionable nightclub."

"Oh, good," Bob said. His expression was serene but resignation filled his voice. "Then we're the patsies. We've got that covered."

Whit reached into an interior pocket of his parka and pulled out his deathmask. The monstrous respirator, large enough to cover the lower two-thirds of his face, was engineered for high-performance air filtering under a broad range of extreme toxic environments. His was designed in a sleek Mesoamerican style to look like the muzzle of a jaguar, all black with snarling matte lips pulled back against gloss fangs. He was pulling it over his head when he noticed his teammates' stares.

"What? Is it my hair?" He shook the dark mop that was brushed up and forward, shellacked into a shaggy wave above his head. "It's at that awkward stage, I know. But there's not really an elegant way of growing out a moh—"

Bob interrupted forcefully. "No."

"It's not your hair," Sakura explained slowly, giving him a perplexed look.

"My suit?" He adjusted the Pratt knot in his narrow duchesse tie and looked down at his ebony worsted wool slacks. "You think it's too conservative."

"Why are you wearing a deathmask to a Johnson meeting?" Bob demanded, glaring at him.

He wilted a little. "Um."

Billy turned away from his watch to see what they were arguing over. "Is that a new team fashion thing?" Billy asked Whit. He pointed toward Bob and Sakura. "Did you guys bring yours, too? Man, I wish I'd known. I didn't bring mine."

"Yeah, that's because you left it in the Rover after last time,"

Sakura told him. "'S okay, it's still there."

Billy gave her a two-handed thumbs-up and resumed monitoring the rooftop across the street.

Whit rubbed his neck, the deathmask perched on his head like the maw of a dyspeptic god that had wandered out of an Aztec codex after a three-day bender of pulque and warrior blood. "It just, you know, seemed like a good idea? I mean, these types go for theatricality and big gestures, right? Besides, it's Eden, so I figured…"

Sakura was still giving him that look.

"They do sound like idiots." Bob nodded in agreement. "They'll probably think you're wizzer."

Sakura sighed. "If these rubes are as cracked as they sound, a little extra leverage with Satan's Johnson might be useful if they get pushy. Facial and vocal masking, with a side order of intimidation?" She pirouetted and struck out across the street. "I guess it's not a totally stupid idea."

Whit related the information that Azcall had given him about the other meeting attendees, and what he personally knew of their respective sects, as the team walked up the spiral staircase to the top floor and the main entrance. The auras Bob had seen belonged to representatives of four of the major Satanist groups in the greater Seattle area.

Members of the Second Church of Satan, Reformed, were mainline Abrahamic conceptually but in practice non-theists. Most lived in corporate citizen enclaves out in the 'burbs. While they publicly repudiated the Homo Puritas Party, in private they would admit to being not particularly keen on the new branches of people that had magically sprouted from the human clade since the elven Sleepers opened the mana dams in the Immanentization decades ago. They couldn't stand the theistic or mystic Satanists, but they loved the pomp and ritual.

In contrast, the Abyssal Nexion was an anarcho-fascist collective that followed a mystic, theistic tradition focused on the sinister feminine archetype. They lived in a compound on the rural fringe of the metroplex and loathed the more urban materialist sects, which they saw as spiritually bankrupt masculinist hegemons. Despite their rejection of patriarchal structures, however, they publicly supported the Puritan political agenda.

The Temple of Black Waters got its start in the Heritage States of America as a petro-cabal following the aftermath of the Great Hub Wipe of 2033, and had spread northward from Dallas. They were atheistic materialists single-mindedly dedicated to radical self-actualization and the disruptive accumulation of capital. They despised the theists and the mystics, as well as traditionalist displays of ritual.

Lastly, the Satanic Fellowship was nontheistic, nonmystical, aggressively nonthreatening, and hated no one—except those who sought to oppress others and hoard knowledge. In fact, tolerance and respectful coexistence with all people, Immanents and otherwise, were among their most treasured values. The other sects universally abhorred them for it but rarely acted or spoke against them because of the Fellowship's notorious expertise in culturejamming and tactical satire.

Then there was Alcime.

"I'm not sure what his interest is in this. Just don't call him a Satanist to his face," Whit whispered as they neared the top of the building.

Billy gave him a confused look. "I thought they were all Satanists?"

"Well—yes. But Alcime is Luciferian. It's…"

Bob paused on a step ahead of them. "So the usual religious schism standards of dumbfuckery still apply, got it." He shook his head impatiently and continued up the last flight of iron steps, breathing heavily.

"Oh, don't say that, either!"

Bob looked over his shoulder in disbelief. "What? 'Dumbfuckery?'"

"No, 'religious.' Half of these people come from a nontheistic magical practice, half are antisocial Amphet junkies with an allergy to social order, and half are committed to prayerful ritual in the desperate hope that Satan-sempai notices them."

"That's a lot of halves," Sakura noted wryly. "You weren't kidding about the factionalization."

"Ehhh, it's more like…there's a lot of overlap?"

"So what's the other 'other' half of the Johnson pan-satanic collective like, then?" Sakura asked.

"They're…" Whit struggled to find the best translation for a layperson. He ran a hand over the human and animal figures intertwined along the iron handrail's surface as he thought. "They're less straightforward."

The team of itakus had reached the head of the line of hopefuls queued at the entrance. The orcs they had seen from the street were still there, now arguing with each other. Up close, Whit could see that the cape was crushed velvet with a scarlet satin lining. He winced inwardly at the man's taste.

"I told you we shouldn't have trusted that elf," hissed the man. He turned his back to the woman and shouted at the troll. "Check again! I am sure our names are on the list."

The orcs were both tall, but the troll easily had another half-meter on them in height. He sighed and spoke in a deep monotone without taking his eyes off his game. "And I'm sure they're not. You can take your turn with the rest of the wannabes, chummer. Or you can make like a tree and go home."

The itakus pushed past the couple and approached the troll. The bouncer examined them, spoke into his throat mic, and then unclipped the glowing rope from a baroque stanchion and waved them inside.

The man in the unfortunate cloak sputtered in outrage. "Why do they get to go inside?" He looked them over and pointed at Bob. "There is no way on earth they are on the list. Did they pay you? I can pay you—"

The woman grabbed his arm. "Come on, it's not worth the bother." She spoke into her comm as she pulled him away and headed back down the walkway. "No, it was a wash. It'll probably turn out to be a fuster cluck anyway. It's a good thing our bank hasn't wired the yunies yet." The man tried to struggle out of her grasp and she smacked him on the back of the head. "Give it a rest, Finicum. Act your age, not your hat size, for frak's sake."

The itakus walked through the entrance, an art-nouveau affair over which *"Qui veggion l'alte creature l'orma de l'etterno valore"* was projected in shimmering gold script. They were met in the lobby by a bald elf with gold cybereyes. She wore a severely cut suit with a geometric pattern woven into the silver cloth. It seemed to suck in light at intervals and gave the silk faille jacket an animated moiré effect.

Whit recognized the lightwell property in the fabric as the hallmark of Hexagram 221Nine, a couture atelier based in Macau. They manufactured their own tubular carbon nanomere cloth, and access to their secretive factory was restricted. Sakura was inspecting the jacket, too, and she grinned when she saw him watching her. *La mode par le main* versus *la mode par l'art* was an ongoing argument between them, Sakura taking the position that remodding clothes through spellcraft was reductionist, ethically bankrupt, and the crutch of a lazy imagination and poor work ethic. Whit defended his practice as being more sustainable, less wasteful, less tedious, and a pity that some people were so jealous.

He mouthed, "I can make that," to her before pulling the deathmask down over his face, and she stifled a laugh.

She messaged his comm:

>**Y100 says you can't**

He sent back:

>**Ur on chummer**

The elf cleared her throat and stared pointedly at the quiver strapped to Billy's hip. "We have a weapons check if the gentlemen or lady would like to secure their belongings."

"That's profiling," Billy said.

"Yeah." Sakura moved to stand next to him. "Pretty gross, chummer."

The elf's golden cybereyes flashed to solid black. "Eden has a strict weapons policy to protect its guests. All of its guests, regardless of race, Immanentization, or ethnicity."

"Then it's a good thing for everyone that we're not guests," Bob said. "We're here on business."

Two imposing men with extensive cyberware stepped out of the shadows. They were dressed in dark suits, with obvious bulges under (and in) the arms of their boxy jackets.

"Please escort these *businesspeople* to their meeting. The one in the Dumah Lounge. Downstairs." The elf gave the itakus a warning look. "Be sure to escort them out of the building through the service tunnel as soon as their himitsu business has concluded. No comps."

"You heard Ms. Eames. Follow me," said one of the muscleboys, who started towards a set of stairs behind the clothing and weapons check. The second muscleboy gestured that the itakus should precede him, then took up a position at their rear as they descended to a tight antechamber containing an iron gate, a four-meter-tall tree, and a very large snake.

The public floors below the entrance were unrestricted territory, but access to the other parts of the club was strictly controlled. A pythian guarded this gate, behind which lay stairs up to the exclusive upper terrace, a lush garden partially open to the sky. The gate and its protector also barred the way to the VIP elevator down to the private rooms at the lowest level, and the discrete entrance that was quietly available at exorbitant cost to patrons who valued privacy more than money.

The pale snake draped over the lower branches of the lignum vitae tree was easily three meters long. It uncoiled, iridescent scales flashing with pinks and blues, and stretched out to block the portal. It assessed each of them with unblinking, sapphire-blue eyes, then nodded to the muscleboy in the lead and recoiled out of their path. It wrapped its thick, pearlescent body around the trunk and moved up to a higher limb to watch them pass.

Billy paused in front of Whit as they followed the others through the gate. He leaned forward without fear and peered closely at the pythian, which cocked its head and flicked its tongue at him.

"That snake is people!" Billy said in an excited whisper when they caught up to the others.

"Probably making minimum wage, if they're even paying her," growled Bob. "Which they probably aren't, if the rumors about Eden trafficking in Immanents are true." His hands balled into fists, and his scowl deepened. "All Immanentized animals still get taken advantage of left and right by people here. And that pythian's young, judging by the size. If she were smart, she'd get the frak out of the metroplex and seek asylum with one of the Council Nations."

Billy wore a thoughtful expression as they followed the muscleboy into the VIP elevator. "I don't know," he said at last. He leaned against the back wall as it descended, and rolled on his shoulder to face Whit. "It depends on which one, you know? It maybe different elsewhere, but snakes aren't too welcome back home, even talking ones."

"Ah, Erskine. You're nearly on time."

Alcime Vannetais stood smiling at the head of a large square table. He had his wheat-blond hair gelled back against his skull and looked to be on the near side of thirty but, given the way elves aged, was likely on the far side of sixty. He wore a narrow gold silk sash across his shoulders, his hands tucked into the trouser pockets of a crisp ebony suit with casual nonchalance. The tie was saffron silk, a shade darker and more orange than the sash, tied in a Windsor knot.

Uncertainty stirred in Whit's stomach, as his experience with Vannetais would suggest neither "casual" nor "nonchalant" to describe him. The episode in the cafe with Azcall was an obvious tipoff that the man had some angle in this, but Whit was still teasing out what it might be. He had a sinking feeling that it was less an angle per se and more of a full geometry whose ultimate form could only be perceived and understood at a remove and from a different vector.

Along the table to Vannetais' right sat two women, clearly representing the Abyssal Nexion. The older of the pair wore faded ballistic nylon coveralls and drummed her fingers on the table in boredom. The other woman, who looked about ten years younger, had wrapped a heavily embroidered shawl over her homespun flannel shirt. They gazed at the itakus with inscrutable expressions.

A young man with a beard and a cheerful face fidgeted next to them. He pulled at the cuffs of the button-down shirt he wore underneath a short-sleeved t-shirt that read *Smile! Satan ❤s You!* That, and the onslaught of earnest goodwill emanating from him were a dead giveaway that he was the emissary from the Satanic Fellowship.

Whit looked their auras in the astral plane. The bearded guy read as mundane, as did the woman in coveralls. Her younger companion was magically active, though. Not at the edge of the magical spectrum—a thresher, like Sakura or Billy—but a full mage. Her aura suggested she was less powerful than him or Bob, but he knew well enough that it could be a ruse. He was in the habit of masking his own aura when out in public or working— like now. He wasn't obscuring that there was a magical signature in his own aura, but he was distorting its unique contour and hiding how powerful it was.

On the other side of the table, nearest Vannetais, was a woman who appeared to be in her early forties. She wore a good-quality navy wool blazer with faint pinstripes, a scarlet tie, and a blue dress shirt with white collar and cuffs. Given the aesthetic rhetoric of serious business being performed, she was probably here to look after the Temple of Black Waters' interests. It wouldn't shock him if the Black Waters had a financial connection to the job's target. They avoided public-relations displays unless one presented them with an opportunity for actionable material advantage. Whit guessed from the distinctive cut of the lapels that the woman's suit was by Rabano, but prêt-à-porter rather than bespoke—a signal that she was still working her way up to the organization's elite. An enamel pin in the form of an eleven-petalled flower surrounded by a black unicursal hexagram was pinned to her left lapel. The ormolu helianthus glowed with an aura when viewed in the astral plane. It was a magical artifact, and it felt like it sustained a low-level spell he couldn't identify. The woman's aura read as mundane but not naturally so. Its contouring was too uniform, its colors flat, like a cartoon parody of what a mundane signature should look like. Whit slowed his breathing as he lightly felt for echoes of the aura hiding behind the cartoon, and smiled with satisfaction when he found them. Her real signature felt magical, like a thresher's, the aura masking probably an effect of the enchanted pin.

Two men sat next to her, one of whom was making an unsubtle display of fiddling with the impractically large and exceptionally ugly analog watch on his wrist. It was gold, with an articulated band of thick links, and an obvious antique from the twentieth century. His adjunct in the Second Church of Satan, Reformed—had to be, with all the other groups accounted for, and who else would be so high-church—was working very hard on appearing indifferent, his eyelids heavy and his gaze directed at his hands resting on the table's top. They were mundane in every sense and thoroughly boring to Whit. They wore red wool cassocks after the Roman style, except the buttons lay on the left-hand side. Of course they did.

Faced with this disparate tableau of fashion power politics,

Whit again regretted not being more semiotically aggressive in his outfit selection. He'd spent the afternoon cycling through a dozen different combinations but had been unsatisfied with any of them. Indecision and second-guessing his choices had left him flustered and unable to concentrate, and made each successive piece that he magically remodded more poorly rendered. He had surrendered in the end to a familiar fallback: the narrow-cut, single-button suit he had crafted so many times that he could remod in his sleep. He sighed and imagined the reaction a more inspired choice might have provoked from the gallery of Johnsons.

Whit was startled out of his sartorial reverie by Sakura elbowing him hard in the ribs. Bob and Billy had sat down in the chairs ahead of them, across the table from Vannetais. Whit played it off with a smirk and pulled out a chair with an exaggerated bow. Sakura rolled her eyes at him. She took the unoccupied chair next to Billy instead, and sat at an angle, keeping an eye on the doorway behind them.

"Erskine? Lambert Erskine? We'd heard you were dead."

His breath caught in his throat. He could feel a thumping flutter below his sternum as sudden fear grabbed him, his heartbeat growing faster and erratic. He whipped his head around to see who had spoken. It was the Johnson from the Church, the one with the gold watch. Under his deathmask, Whit struggled to keep calm while he tried to rein in the panic pressing down on his chest.

"You're looking well! I'm so pleased to see we were ill-informed.

It's such a pleasure to—"

Vannetais broke in smoothly. "No, Horace. You're thinking of Erskine the elder. This is Erskine the younger."

"Oh." The ingratiating smile fell from the man's batrachian face. "Pity."

Whit considered casting a mana spike at Horace, then decided he would be better served with setting his face on fire, given the current company. His fight-or-flight response was quelled by Vannetais catching his eye with a subtle shake of his head. Whit started when he realized that his emotional state was probably bleeding through his aura masking. It was dumb and dangerous, letting the mention of his father get to him like that. No one had seen Lambert in over five years, despite the bounties on his head for murder and embezzlement. Even his own lawyers thought he was probably dead, although the will stipulated it could not be executed without proof of death. Not that it mattered, he hadn't left much estate to execute. Lambert had burned through several fortunes to support his magical artifact obsession. Whit took a deep breath and sat down, trying to refocus his self-control. Sakura leaned behind Billy's wide, muscular back and raised an inquisitive eyebrow at him, which he ignored.

The elf redirected the conversation back to the job. "We did not convene today to play host to your fatuous arriviste displays, Horace."

"Quite so," said the woman in flannel. Her companion slid her

DeWitt Wilcox

eyes away from the assembled team of itakus to the man Vannetais had called out, and her lip curled in disgust. The men from the Church pretended not to notice but looked everywhere around the room except at the Abyssal Nexion's representatives.

"Right!" The bearded Johnson from the Satanic Fellowship rubbed his hands together and looked around the table. "Now that we're all here, we can get down to business."

Alcime sat down and crossed his legs. He gestured for him to continue.

The bearded man ducked his head in acknowledgment. "First, I'd like to thank everyone for putting aside past disagreements and coming together today in service of a greater goal." At this, the Johnson from the Black Waters eyed Horace and his cassocked counterpart sidelong and clenched her jaw, but didn't interrupt. "And I'd like to extend a warm welcome to our guests. Hail Satan," the Fellow said with a perky smile as he flashed devil horns with his left hand.

Billy raised his fist in kind. "Hail Satan!" He yelped when Bob kicked him under the table. "Ow!" He turned to the mage. "What was that for?"

Bob shrugged. "Sorry. My foot slipped."

The Fellow fluttered his hands in the air as he sent data to the room's secure holoprojection node. A series of media files unwrapped themselves to hang in a polygonal carousel formation above the middle of the table.

The woman in flannel put her hand up to interrupt his presentation. She challenged the itakus with a long stare. "You are all magically active."

Her companion from the Abyssal Nexion shifted her gaze back to the itakus, and the corners of her mouth twitched. The other Johnsons looked at Vannetais, who nodded, unperturbed.

Sakura returned her stare. "And argon's a noble gas. What's your point?"

"It is unusual," the Black Waters Johnson murmured.

"Isn't that bad luck?" The second Johnson from the Church knitted his eyebrows in concern. He turned to Horace next to him. "I heard that was bad luck, to let too many merlins get together."

"Well, technically, not everyone who is magically active is also a mage," the Fellow said.

The Black Waters Johnson tsked under her breath. She started to say something to the itakus but the woman in flannel interrupted her.

"'Too many mages?'" she growled at the two Church Johnsons across the table. "Which of us here would you have eliminated?"

The Black Waters Johnson glanced at Vannetais, then back at Horace and Not-Horace. She moved her chair further down the table, away from the cassocked men. "Good luck with that," she said to them.

Horace placed a hand on his chest as alarm stole over his face. He reached out to his left without actually touching the other

Johnson from the Church. "What my associate means is that, in regards to itakus, a team composed exclusively of, ah, magical types, might possibly be somewhat…asymmetrical?"

"The mundane ignoramus has a point," said the Black Waters Johnson. Not-Horace sputtered with indignation, but Horace peremptorily shushed him when she sneered at them. She then nodded at the itakus and continued, "Is that all you bring to the table? What about electronic systems? Matrix infiltration? Smuggling? Close-quarters combat?"

"I can punch spirits in the face," Billy said. His pleasant, matter-of-fact tone suggested he were picking up a lunch order rather than pitching himself as a stone-cold criminal operative.

"We have a rolling drone rigger, and an ace hacker," Sakura said. Bob coughed behind his hand at this. She ignored him. "As well as access to heavy conventional firepower. We get the job done."

Whit followed up. "It would help to know what the job is, of course."

"Yes." Vannetais took control of the meeting once again. Whit thought he saw mischief in the lingering study the elf gave him before his face settled back into an uncharacteristic mask of placid amiability. "That is customary in these arrangements." He gestured to the Fellow. "If you would continue, please."

"Right! Of course." The Fellow ducked his head again. He turned to address the itakus. "You may have heard about the unpleasantness in the news," he began. "But in the wake of the

Everett Possession Massacre, Boeing-Marubeni announced a new diversity initiative to reduce workplace tensions and generally improve employee morale at their Everett campus. Part of that initiative was the Celebration of Wisdom." He swiped his hand in the air, and the file carousel rotated. A silent video of a sculpture garden began playing in the primary field of view.

"And that was great. Even better, Boeing-Marubeni agreed to employee requests to include a statue of the divine androgyne Baphomet among the representations of the sages."

"The Dark Goddess," intoned the woman in flannel. "The Culler of Men."

"You mean the hieroglyph of arcane perfection, of course," interjected Horace.

"The Sabbatic Goat," said the suit from the Black Waters, talking over them both.

The atmosphere in the room grew tense once more as the representatives of the different sects seethed at each other. Whit felt a sudden change in the ambient mana as someone—he thought it was the Abyssal Nexion mage—started to stealth-cast. He began to activate his magical defenses in expectation of getting caught in the crossfire when Alcime cleared his throat with enough force to attract the disputants' collective attention.

"By whichever avatar one recognizes the thoughtform known as Baphomet, we can all agree that including it in a public corporate display was a welcome and progressive move."

The Fellow exhaled with relief at this interruption. The mana vibration in the room stilled, although the mage from the Abyssal Nexion gave Alcime a dark look. He blithely ignored this and instead focused on the Fellow.

"As you were saying?"

"Um, yeah." The Fellow stammered as he tried to reboard his train of thought. "Right! So, everything was great until they unveiled the installation." He gestured with pinched fingers toward the video playing above the table. As he expanded them, the image re-centered and zoomed in to a goat-headed statue.

"Abomination," the woman in coveralls said through clenched teeth.

"Ridiculous," moaned Horace.

"Not really canon," said the Black Waters suit, with a disappointed shrug.

The Fellow opened his arms wide in recognition of the consensus. He turned to the itakus with an expectant if rueful smile. "You can see the problem. We need you to fix it."

The itakus looked at each other and tried to hide their confusion as consultation. Whit caught Bob's eye and twitched his eyebrows in an unspoken question. Bob snorted and gave a dismissive shake of his head.

"Wait, so they put the wrong statue on display? Is it because they stuck the goat's head on a man's body?" asked Billy, whose education to this point had not included the finer points of

Hermetic iconographic history.

Bob looked at the Johnsons. "Fix what, exactly?"

Alcime's left eyebrow twitched up a fraction. The woman from the Black Waters snickered. The other Johnsons stared at the itakus with respective measures of shock, disappointment, and disapprobation.

Not-Horace leaned forward and steepled his fingers. "We want you to correct the statue to its proper archetypal manifestation," he explained. "Obviously."

The room was silent as the itakus first looked at him, and then at each other. Billy and Sakura exchanged uncertain expressions while Bob closed his eyes and pinched the bridge of his nose. Whit looked back at the Johnsons.

"So," he began, glad the deathmask hid the incredulous grin that he couldn't quite tamp down. "Did you have a particular cup size in mind?"

Billy did a quick double-take and looked at the Johnsons with suspicion.

Sakura tilted her head. "You really mean—"

"They want us to put tits on it," Bob said. He dropped his hand from his face and looked up at the Johnsons. "I have that right? You're upset they installed a statue of Baphomet without the standard factory equipment?"

Across the table, Alcime leaned back and rested his chin on his hand, not bothering to hide a sly smile as he curled his index finger lightly across his lips.

"It's more complicated than that," said the woman in flannel. She adjusted her shawl around her shoulders. "But…"

"Yes!" The other representative from the Abyssal Nexion interrupted, to her companion's visible bemusement. After a pause she cleared her throat and leaned back. "It's exactly that."

"Well, that was an exceptionally ludicrous display of internecine nonsense," Whit groused as they walked out of a rear service entrance onto the alley behind Eden. He shoved the door open with too much force, and it sent the magically generated cloudbank on the outside spiraling away. He caught the door as it rebounded off a dumpster with a clang and held it open for the others behind him.

Sakura called out from the back. "Shiny side up, isn't that how we figured it would go?"

"Man, did you guys catch a look at the scarf that elf was wearing? That thing was lit as frak on the astral," Billy said as he passed Whit.

"Oh, that." Whit shrugged. "Yeah, it's woven from Danaë spider silk."

"I'd like to know by who." Bob glanced at him as he walked past through the doorway. "If that was what I think it was."

Sakura pursed her mouth in curiosity at Bob's back as she

exited behind him. "What do you think it was?"

"Spiritcloth. Put out one helluva of an aura, I'll tell you."

She shook her head. "It's got to be a fake."

Whit threw back his head and laughed.

She gave him an irritated look. "I mean, even a fake like that has got to be expensive. Don't get me wrong—the weave was gorgeous, but that was not an 'Atło original."

"No, it wasn't." Whit nodded in agreement as he let go of the door. "I mean, I've never seen anything by 'Atło, not in person, anyway, but I'm pretty sure that didn't come out of Four Corners. Too obvious for Alcime's taste."

"Who's 'Atło?" asked Billy. "The name sounds Navajo."

"An eigengeist," Bob replied. He started walking down the alley, toward the street where they'd met up earlier. "And a free citizen of the Four Corners Council."

"Huh," Billy said.

"'Atło makes this amazing magical clothing," Sakura explained as they followed Bob. "They're famous for it. But they don't make many pieces, and the ones they do are total cash sinks. Like, there was a lot of buzz about 'Atło making a robe for some elf *arphen*, and it supposedly cost more yunies than I've ever made. Combined. I mean, by an order of magnitude."

Billy gave Whit an inquiring look over his shoulder. "Are all your other friends that fancy?"

Whit kicked at an empty beer bottle lying on the ground,

missed, and swore. "He's not a friend! He's just this guy who—you know what? Doesn't matter." He flexed his fingers in agitation. "Whatever. And, technically, it's not a scarf. It's a pallium."

"Okay," Billy said patiently. "So, it's a really expensive scarf."

Whit shrugged, his attention distracted by a staccato burst of pink neon light from the club's roof. It reflected off the darkened windows above the alley and was scattered by the clouds. He looked behind them, in the astral as well as the material plane, checking to make sure no one had followed them from the club. "I'm sure it cost him a lot, just not in cash. Services, favors, life force, maybe. The types of spirits he works with aren't much interested in money or material affairs, as such."

Sakura tapped Billy on the shoulder. "Or maybe the guy nicked it. He can't be that legit if he gets involved in itaku business openly." She gave Whit an artful smirk. "You can see it, right? Like, maybe he hustled it from an eigengeist, or from someone who got it legit?" She nudged Billy's arm conspiratorially. "Bet he'd be wiz at the grift."

Whit groaned as he caught up to them. Of all the things she could have picked about the absurd meeting, trust Sakura to pounce on something he didn't want to discuss. "I don't know why you guys are obsessing over him. Actually…" He stopped melodramatically, as though a thought had struck him. He stared at them with theatrical seriousness. "I think I do. You know spiritcloth has enchantments woven into it? Usually a glamour?

Often with an implicit compulsion, or fostering an obsession with the wearer?" He leaned forward. "Sound familiar?"

"I don't think we're the ones who've been glamoured," she said, pointing to herself and Billy.

"Who's been glamoured?" Billy asked her.

Whit regretted making the joke. It had just made things worse on an already crappy night. "No one's been glamoured!"

"Yeah. Could be," Sakura drawled. "Maybe we're interested because you're being extra weird about this."

"I am not!" He threw up his hands. "I don't know why you people think I hang out with him on weekends playing Tarocchino, or something."

Bob called from the end of the alley. "Could we continue this tomorrow in a more appropriate venue?"

"Yes!" Whit agreed testily. He stalked past them. "Or, not continue it at all."

"What the frak is Tarocchino?" Sakura yelled at his back.

Whit was waiting by the Rover when Sakura 2000 caught up to him. He leaned against the building next to the oversize vehicle, his arms crossed, one foot tucked under him on the wall at an angle.

"Hoi, did ya need something?" Her tone was cool.

He reached inside an interior coat pocket and pulled out a

pack of cigarettes. He flipped open the box with his thumb, then shook one out and lit it magically.

"Tarocchino is a card game." When she didn't respond, he continued, "You play with tarot cards, in pairs. It's kind of like Minchiate." He took a drag off his cigarette. "Or like euchre, or bridge?" He flicked ash into the gutter and gazed up at the naturally occurring cloud cover. The wind had picked up while they were inside, and it was thinning in wisps against the night sky. "But different. Obviously."

"Billy'll be disappointed to hear that. He bet me fifty yunies that it's 'one of those fancy synthcaf drinks.'"

Whit chuckled, but his smile faltered when he saw the stony expression on Sakura's face. She crossed her arms and tapped her toe expectantly.

Oh.

"Is this about the alley?" he ventured.

She cocked her head toward him.

"Or, more specifically, any irritability I might have directed— regrettably and unjustly—at my esteemed colleagues while traversing through said alley?"

She nodded but gestured for him to continue.

He squinted. "And … my lamentable wardrobe choices for this evening?"

She rolled her head back and groaned. "No, not that."

"For which I also apologize sincerely?"

Sakura took a step closer and looked him in the eye. The stacked heels of her pumps made her almost as tall as he was. "Not that I object on moral grounds to nuking the Johnson, but I got to draw the line at doing it before they pay us. What the frak was with you tonight?"

"I never!" His mouth fell open in indignation. He snapped it shut at the genuine concern in her frown.

"I've worked with you for two years, Whit. I think I've sussed the signs when you're about to melt some frakker's face off."

"I was not!" He tried to ignore his reaction to Horace and failed. "I…okay, maybe I did give the idea some brief but earnest consideration. The way things unfolded tonight." He took a half turn away, to put more space between them. "It pushed my buttons in a way I didn't expect. I'm sorry. I am an unprofessional idiot."

"Yeah, well." She studied him for a moment, then dropped her arms with a conciliatory sweep. The tension in the air dissipated. "If you were a professional idiot, we'd all probably be dead by now."

Whit gave her a chagrined half-smile. He wasn't sure if she meant the ribbing as a compliment or an indictment, but he took it as a peace offering. "Uh, I need a ride. I mean, can, *may* I get a ride. Please?"

"Oh, for frak's sake, Whit. I don't know why you don't buy your own car, and just leave it in autonomous mode to drive you around." She put her hands on her hips, then sighed as she deactivated the active defense systems. "Yeah, of course, get in. And put that thing out first."

"That's what friends and public transportation are for. I'm performing a public service by not adding to traffic. Besides, riding alone would be a downer." He opened the rear passenger door and took a deep pull on his cigarette. He was about to drop it in the gutter and climb into the truck when the itaku rigger spoke again.

"For 'just some guy,' Alcime seems to know you pretty well, huh."

Whit glared at her over the roof of the truck, but he relented at her evil grin. She may have accepted his apology, but her curiosity wasn't going to let him off without some satisfaction. He sighed and gazed up. A circular Seattle's Next-Best Security hoverdrone passed far overhead on a subscription patrol route.

"Not that well," he mumbled, and he heard her snort with disbelief. He glanced over at her. She was watching him with sly interest once again.

"I don't! I mean, he doesn't." He rolled his shoulders back. "I'm not being weird about anything!"

Sakura didn't reply, but her eyebrows crept farther up.

"Stop that. Look, he's like, forty years older than I am. I'm only on his radar because he was an external advisor on my senior thesis in college. I needed someone with a background in Enochian to get it approved, and you know, it's a small pool to choose from."

She hummed. He inhaled on the dwindling cigarette for a heartbeat too long to pass the pause off as indifference. He exhaled smoke through tight lips. "And our paths sometimes cross at events around town. Like I said."

"Uh-huh. 'Magical town is small town.' I got that part." She stepped up on the running board and leaned her elbows on the roof. "So, speaking of small town, we need to talk about that 'Erskine the elder' business."

"Ahh, ah-ah-ah, not talking about that." Whit wagged a finger at her. Her poking him about Alcime was one thing, but his immediate family history was a hot zone whose perimeter he would not breach. "Not relevant to work."

Sakura wrinkled her nose in frustration. "It's relevant if it means your cover isn't solid. It's relevant if your secret identity is not-in-any-frakking-way secret!"

"It's steganography. I'm hiding in plain sight."

"Do you have any idea how steganography actually works? That's ridiculous, even for you." Sakura reached down and opened the driver's door.

"No!" he insisted. "It's wiz. I'm my own fake identity. Anyone who tags me will assume that I've stolen this sucker's ID. It won't occur to them that I am, in fact, he. If I catch any heat, all I have to do is play dumb, and they'll think I'm the sucker instead of the brilliant itaku. Besides." He took a last drag off the cigarette and flicked the stub over his shoulder. It flared and was consumed by spellfire before it could hit the sidewalk. "I'm magic." He grinned and slid into the passenger compartment.

Chapter 3

T HE JOHNSONS HAD SET THE deadline for the job's completion by the Boeing-Marubeni Everett campus' nondenominational holiday party on December 20, the eve of the winter solstice. That gave the itakus three days to scout the location, fabricate a set of suitable mammaries, and devise and execute a plan for infiltration, installation, and evacuation.

Whit had taken the monorail down from the stop closest to his apartment on the eastern slope of Phinney Ridge to a run-down neighborhood on the far south side of the metroplex's urban core, where they had a tiny safe house. Bob had set it up in an empty storefront that shared the alley behind his low-cost spay-and-neuter clinic so that the team could plan their jobs more efficiently and "keep you assholes out of my hair" at the clinic, despite his never seeming to have any clients.

During the ride, Whit had replayed the meeting in his head. He had to admit that his defensiveness the night before was irrational and unprofessional, even by loose itaku standards. After all, the job was kind of funny, conceptually, and only a fool argued against having yunies in hand. That being said, at only fifteen thousand, it wasn't paying as well as he had expected. Their most recent jobs had promised nearly twice that (though not always delivered upon completion). This job increasingly bothered him the more he thought about it. What he had told Sakura last night was true, but it was more than the bad vibes generated by the social dynamics and enmity among the Johnsons or his personal baggage. It was hard for him to articulate what didn't feel right, which further fed his vexation.

"This is below our pay grade," he grumbled. He slouched over a backwards chair in the safe house's secure back room. "And also stupid."

"Reality check: you're getting fifteen thousand yunies—ten of those up front, thanks to Bob's negotiating—to pull off what's basically a dumb prank. People pay for stupid," Sakura replied. "Don't worry—it's the serious jobs that always frak us over."

"Boy howdy." Billy was pacing around the room upside-down in a handstand. "Like the one last year when we were supposed to extract that chemical engineer from Avalon, and the 'soft the Johnson gave us to erase the exit logs melted the plant's reactor instead."

Whit dropped his chin on the back of the chair and closed his eyes. "And we never saw it coming. We should have."

"We trusted the wrong hacker." Billy kicked out of his handstand. He looked up as he brushed his hands off on his thighs. "Live and learn."

"Milkboy told us it was a solid melt for the prime node's ICE." Sakura looked at Whit with commiseration. "He lied about the code audit he ran on the soft before slotting it."

"Jinx!" Billy said. "You said his name. Next time we're out, the first round is on you."

"That's fair."

Whit raised his head. "Prank war or no, I still think this job is a waste of our talents."

Bob entered from the alley side-passage and glanced over at Whit as he secured the false wall behind himself. His brow furrow crawled up his forehead as he scrutinized them. "You're the one who set this up. Maybe you need better friends."

"They are not my friends," Whit said. "And I didn't 'set up' this job. It just got dropped in my lap. Not sure how our names floated to the top of the pile or why Alcime is personally involving himself…"

"Does it matter?" Bob crossed his arms and regarded him coldly. "There's always a how and why in any job, but they all boil down to the same thing: Johnsons have a problem, we fix it for money."

"Besides, Johnsons are all chancy baggers in the first place, or they wouldn't be hiring itakus." Sakura wrinkled her chin a little when she saw the faint frown pass quickly over Whit's face. "No offense. I mean, you don't trust any of them, right?"

"Of course not." There was a spectrum of Johnson reliability, to be sure, but they were all dangerous to some degree. The professionals, who handled business for corps, legit or otherwise, would sell their itakus out in a heartbeat if it fulfilled requirements or gave them an edge over the jerk in the next office. The individuals and small businesses at the other end, mostly amateurs, endangered themselves and their itakus with their sloppiness and naïveté.

"Alcime included?" she asked.

"Well, no. I don't trust him, per se." He didn't intend that to sound so defensive. "But I don't have any reason to not trust him."

Bob's lower lip jutted out in a parody of thoughtfulness. "Except that he told you to take a job from people he obviously hates."

"What happened to 'all jobs boil down to the same thing?'" he asked skeptically.

"Just pointing out that trust isn't what gets us paid." Bob threw up his hands in defeat. "Trust him, or don't. I honestly don't give a frak. Just so long as it doesn't get in the way of fixing the problem."

"Or of getting paid," Sakura added.

"If something is bothering you, you could ask him?" Billy said diplomatically. "I learn all sorts of things when I ask."

"C'mon, Whit," Sakura said. "It's not like this is the dumbest job we've ever taken. Compare it to the retired UW professor?"

"The one we babysat for a week while she tried to complete that ritual?"

Billy shook his head in disbelief. "And after all that work to get immortal youth, she ended up turning into a statue."

"Without paying us first. Unforgivable." Bob growled. "And where the frak is that 'Original Itaku' guy? I can't get him on the comm. Probably because I deleted his number," he admitted.

Sakura pinged The Original Itaku on the team's shared channel, but the hacker's parasoft agent responded instead:

>The Original Itaku is:
processing in an alt.er.net node
Contact ID: (confirmed) chummer ichiban
Accept file transfer: "BoeMaru_Ev_fac_dump"? [y/n]

"Still defragging his drek, looks like," she said. "He sent something. It'll spam out to you after the transfer request clears my decon agent."

"The theoretical underpinnings of the spellcraft involved with the professor's plan were quite provocative," mused Whit. "It was shame they didn't quite translate into practice." Once it had become clear payment would not be forthcoming, ever, Bob had requisitioned the magical contents of her lab for his own secretive experiments. Sakura, Billy, and himself had kept the successfully rejuvenated but unfortunately lithified body as payment in kind for their portion. They installed it in their magical lodge, where the statue did double-duty as ritual altar and coatrack. The talk of the late professor reminded him the three of them hadn't yet decided on a theme for their lodge's winter solstice party.

"You got to admit that the new Johnsons' statue would be better with boobs," Billy said. "Even though those guys were annoying."

"Yeah, they were," agreed Sakura. She leaned toward Whit. "I still wanna know what that 'Erskine the elder' business was all that about," she whispered.

Whit crossed his arms. "It's nothing."

"Was he a Satanist, too?" She elbowed him in the arm. "Is that what's got you acting so unhinged? Embarrassed about the old man's goofer religion?"

"Gods, no," he hissed at her. "You're the one who's unhinged." He shook his head at the thought of Lambert indulging in anything so comparatively sentimental.

"Is that your dad?" Billy asked. He did a backflip and landed next Sakura without a sound. "He has a funny name."

Whit glared at a blank spot on the wall above his teammates' heads and ignored them.

"As fascinating as Whit's mysterious past isn't, can we get back to planning before he burns a hole in my safe house?" Bob opened the location information The Original Itaku had sent, and threw it up on the display laminate that covered most of the back wall.

"This remote hacker thing is bushwa. We could really use The Orig's infiltration chops on the ground with this," Sakura said. "I wonder what he's got cooking on the backend. I bet it's Flatline 'business.' No way that bar he opened is legit."

"It totally looks like an itaku bar," Billy said, his voice full of admiration. "They sell t-shirts with their matrix plot and everything, too."

"More like an itaku bar in a kids' show," scoffed Sakura. "Or for tourists."

"Verified. I took out-of-plex friends there once. They loved it," Whit said as he flipped through the files in AR on his goggles. "We need to get a more reliable hacker on the team. I like the guy, but … he's kind of like a cat?"

"Wanders in, hangs out, wanders out. Probably has three other families in the village feeding him?" said Billy.

"Plays with string and licks his own balls?" Bob looked at them, then waved his hand in the direction of the clinic. "Not after coming to me, obviously."

Sakura wrinkled her nose as they were reminded of their previous hacker. "Ew. And I thought that Milkb—that guy did that to himself."

Bob held up his hands. "Hey! Just engaging in some observational humor. I got no responsibility for that dickless piece of nullo hacker drek. Except for helping to shoot him into space to almost-certain death."

"Best decision we ever made," Sakura murmured. Her eyes flicked back and forth as she scanned the files that fed directly in through her datalink. She turned to Whit. "Hey, doesn't Major

Label have someone she could recommend? I'm assuming she has better things to do than slum with us, but…"

"Yeah, she's a legit Elflands citizen." Whit hummed in the back of his throat as he thought it over. His best friend from college was a phenomenal hacker, but she had stayed in Portland to work for a non-profit after they graduated. She'd be even less available for on-site work than The Orig. "I can ask if there's anyone on her radar. She's got feelers all over, in some pretty random places."

"Focus, please," barked Bob.

"Jeez, Bob, relax. We are. Maybe you need to lay off the stims? Take a nap?" Sakura said in an even tone as she took comm control of the display.

Whit leaned his chest against the back of the chair and chewed his lip as Sakura ran down her recon plan for the perimeter operations at the Everett facility. His mind started to wander when she got to predictive security algorithms, and he considered Billy's earlier suggestion. He hesitated, then furtively typed out a message to Alcime:
>**Why?**

The answer came swiftly:
>**It amuses me, on many levels.**

That was obvious, but the vagueness there hinted there was something more coiled under the surface. He poked again:
>**And hiring us?**

The response came more slowly this time:

>**You are the ideal candidates for what is required.**

He sighed and set his comm's intercept agent so that it wouldn't interrupt him while they worked out plans for the job. Bob was right: he did need to focus, and Alcime clearly wasn't keen to tip his hand to whatever it was that he was getting out of this absurd enterprise. Maybe he was reading too much into it, and the elven mage was just in it for the schadenfreude. A front-row seat to witness the metroplex's least-likely-to-get-along esoteric community forced to play nice with each other, all in the holiday spirit of goat-person breast augmentation? Whit would be the first to acknowledge that, as magical "small town" spectacles went, it was a fun, harmless farce.

And as for his team's involvement with it, well. Someone had to play Santa. It might as well be them.

"How do you want to handle the boobs?" Bob looked tired despite their late-morning start.

Billy snorted with laughter next to Whit. After an initial round of jokes following the Johnson meeting, the rest of the team had become inured to the entendre-related perils inherent to the current job. Billy was the youngest by a couple of years, however, and refused to be burdened by their urbane ennui.

"We don't have time for traditional fine-art methods," Sakura said. "The easiest way is going to be printing them from mesh geometry. I can make breast models scaled to the statue's measurements, pull a matching mineralogical profile from the 'trix to sinter, then fab them in my workshop."

"What about welding them on? The Johnsons weren't explicit, but it would be nice if the new rack were impossible to remove," Whit said.

"We need to match the stone." Sakura shook her head. "Plus, too much operational weight. We'd have to get the welding gear to the location, set it up, and do the work without raising suspicion. The finished result would look janky if we get rushed. But plus-one on the future-proofing." She tapped her teeth with a fingernail while she pondered their options. The hue on the lacquer shifted in spectrum from blue to violet and back with each touch. "I'm thinking concealed steel anchors and mil-spec adhesive. There's an instant marine epoxy that environmental response forces use for repairs on tankers and pipes on derricks at sea. It's designed to work in wet conditions, even underwater, but it does the trick in air above fifty-percent humidity, too. So, with Seattle's usual weather…" She shrugged. "We should be all right."

"Getting on the corporate campus might be problematic." Bob frowned at the data The Original Itaku had sent. "Boeing-Marubeni does a lot of classified government work for the Con-Fed in Everett, but this says they're just as paranoid about their own commercial projects. Eighty percent of the staff lives on campus, and permeability of the outer perimeter is controlled by RFID access badge."

"Biometrics?"

"Only for the regular staff and residents. Contractors have fingerprints on record, but for non-sensitive staff they're only used to validate their access cards, which is idiotic."

"No two-factor scanning?" Sakura examined the data more closely and incredulity bloomed on her face. "That's a hella dumb unit test model."

Whit started, "What does th—"

"A prole just needs to have their fingerprint match the one on their access card," she explained. "It's the card that gets read by the perimeter and internal checks, not the meat, so if we can get that spoofed, we're on."

"No way it's that easy," he said.

"The Orig should be able to get us replica access cards with promiscuous biometric pairing. We're good as long as he can also spoof the card authentication." Sakura waved a hand. "They're relying on strong encryption and anticipating sophisticated systematic attacks. Big corporate sec often overlooks small, fiddly meatspace threats. They're worried about wolves. Ants aren't their problem. That's for a different department to deal with."

Bob nodded. "That's the responsibility of the tactical security patrols. They'll know the regular patterns and behavior for residents. We need a plausible external cover."

"A marching band!" Billy clapped his hands and rubbed them together. "Or statue cleaners?"

Seized with inspiration, Whit snapped his fingers. "We go in as the art consultants. One of us poses as the sculptor, overseeing the installation of their magnum opus, which the corporate slugs obviously botched and which needs to be corrected. Someone else is the artist's agent or maybe the gallery owner." He paused while he considered the dramatic exigencies of the role. "That's probably me. Then the rest of the team are the studio assistants."

"Who do the actual labor?" asked Sakura. Her eyes narrowed.

"Well, yeah."

"Then I'm the artist," Sakura said decisively. She turned and pointed towards Bob and Billy. "You two are the studio assistants."

"Why do you get to be the artist? You're stronger than I am. You should do the heavy lifting," Bob argued.

"Yeah, and I can be the gallery owner!" exclaimed Billy.

"No," Bob and Sakura said in near-unison.

"That would make Whit a studio assistant," she said.

"And he can't lift drek," Bob said.

"Hey!" he objected.

CHAPTER 4

BOB SAT ALONE INSIDE THE warded biocontainment lab hidden under his discount spay-and-neuter clinic. He pulled away from the microscope with a yawn and rubbed his eyes with the back of his hand. The stims he'd taken were wearing off. He glanced at the time. 02:00. One more sample left to process tonight, then he could hit the sack. This was the last of the experimental specimens he had tried to artificially shock into magical activation, but signs so far indicated it hadn't taken. He slid the slide under the scope. Same as the others: no visible histological change to reflect an increased sensitivity to mana. He removed the sample and placed it into the thaumaturgic spectrometer to be scanned at the molecular level.

If his condition had been a known mundane disease, then finding a matching donor through conventional channels might have been difficult, certainly expensive, but at least it would have been conceivably possible. None of the oncologists he consulted had seen a magically active leukemia like his before, however, let alone had any clue how to treat it. Their initial tests suggested it would not respond to the chemo and gene therapy treatments typically used for the closest mundane variety. His checkered past made it impossible to seek experimental treatment elsewhere under his real identity, and the unique nature of the disease made it unsafe to risk it under an assumed one, so he decided to treat himself. He had a medical degree and clinical experience, and best of all, no institutional review board to breathe down his neck and interfere.

One upside to working itaku jobs was its supply of generally young and somewhat healthy research subjects who could disappear without anyone noticing. On the off chance someone did notice one of these poor saps had vanished, they probably didn't care, and if they cared, they weren't in a position to do anything about it. The team frequently crossed paths with gangers, rent-a-thugs, and dime-a-dozen cogs in the megacorp machinery who didn't walk away from those encounters. Bob recognized they were a resource from day one. He sold off the bodies he couldn't use for his experiments to organ-leggers after stripping them of cyberware, which he also sold if it were in good condition or recyclable. Getting the bodies back to his lab was a problem, until he worked out a profit-sharing arrangement with Sakura 2000 to haul them back in her truck after jobs. He'd offered to split the proceeds among the whole team. Billy had shrugged and said he didn't care, while Whit openly objected, as if he didn't drop half the mooks with kill spells in the first place. Their old hacker had taken a cut, but Bob hadn't mentioned the arrangement to the new guy. No sense in rocking that boat.

He pushed back from the lab bench and stroked his stubbled chin in thought while the sample processed. The best treatment option he had modeled needed a close leukocyte antigen match in a magically active donor. The antigen match was the relatively easy part. Easy, that is, if he used corporate tissue banks, but those were officially closed to someone with his profile. Bribing his way in via a back door would have been an option if he had the social connections. He didn't. The underground tissue banks that the organ-leggers supplied were hit-or-miss on quality, and the chances of getting accurately typed, fresh, viable transplant tissue from them were wafer-thin at best. Still, the antigen match was a solvable problem.

The crux of the problem was finding a match within his own mana-sensitivity group. He'd found mundanes with several of the right leukocyte antigen markers, but experimental results showed that wouldn't suffice. Donor cells or marrow would have to come from someone who was fully magically active. Someone on the threshold wouldn't fit the bill. It would have to come from another mage.

Trouble was, there weren't many of those in the general population, and fewer still among the class of bodies he ran into while on itaku jobs. Sure, in a random sample of a random group of 1,000,000 people, you'd find 10,000 who were magic in some way, and at least one thousand of those would be full mages. But the metroplex wasn't a random group once it got sliced into corps and gangs and other institutional siphons that sucked in valuable assets like mages. In addition, those organizations noticed when non-disposable assets went missing, and they got aggressive when it came to repossessing them. The relatively few unaffiliated mages, who hadn't been recruited, kidnapped, or otherwise collected, were generally either untrained and too hard to identify, or too powerful for anyone sane to mess with.

He'd tried to solve this piece of the treatment problem by taking mundane basal humans and trying to force their bodies into a magically active state. This had turned out to be a dead-end, based on the research he could do in secret with the resources he had. His earliest attempts on live subjects had resulted in their going mad and tearing themselves (and his lab) apart while he was away at a Johnson meeting. He then narrowed the scope with this most recent experiment, to magically activate mundane blood and tissue samples rather than entire organisms. He had hypothesized that the metaphysical nature of magic could operate more powerfully on a synecdoche than a whole, but the results so far did not support this.

He yawned and let his eyes stay closed to rest, just for a second. The thaumaturgic spectrometer beeped, and he jerked upright.

02:42, now. He'd fallen asleep while the sample processed. He leaned over to check the results on the display panel. Another failure, confirming his visual assessment and consistent with the molecular results for the previous samples in the batch. He would have to start from scratch and keep searching for a suitable mage donor, or find a new experimental avenue.

He had made the initial assumption that a donor would also need to be within his own Immanentization branch. But maybe this assumption was wrong. Basal humans were, generally speaking, less mana-sensitive than the recent branches that had sprouted after the ley dams fell and mana flooded the world decades ago. The Immanentized branches, including orcs, trolls, and most elves, originated from those humans so sensitive to mana that it transmogrified their genetic code, like a magical CRISPR run amuck. That increased sensitivity might be retained in those populations, even among mundane individuals. While his mundane basal human specimens didn't respond to forced activation, perhaps a specimen from one of these hereditary Immanentized populations would. It would also expand his pool of potential donor candidates by a good thirty percent or so. At a minimum, assessing experimental samples outside of the basal human clade would help test and refine his working hypothesis regarding mana sensitivity as a required donor characteristic.

Bob initiated the low-power mode sequence for the equipment on the bench. He stood up and winced at the pinch in his lower back and the dull ache in his hips. He shook his head as he headed up to the shabby apartment above his clinic. It was too bad he had to conduct his research on the down-low. It would have made for some stellar conference papers.

TUESDAY
18 DECEMBER, 2074

3 DAYS UNTIL WINTER SOLSTICE

CHAPTER 5

T HE ROVER SAT IN A commuter lot at Everett Station, partially obscured by a large elm. Sakura watched a maglev train pull out of the station from her command rig in the sealed driver's compartment. As it accelerated, the train's blunt needle nose cut through the morning's drifting mists of rain. The mosaic of random lights on its sides blurred, then as it reached speed resolved through persistence of vision into advertisements for a new NeuroSim romantic comedy starring Bwiimbrin the Skunk Ape. She checked the passenger compartment vid feed. Whit was sprawled across the middle seat, feet up on the far door. She couldn't see his eyes through the blacked-out goggles strapped to his head, but the slackness in his face suggested the mage was still out, doing his eerie astral projection thing.

She shifted her focus back to the S2K-Tombo minidrone she was flying, and the truck's cabin feed automatically minimized in her optical display. She built most of her drones herself, including the S2K-Tombo. It had the form of a tigertail dragonfly, though the drone was slightly larger to accommodate the necessary electronics. It possessed 360° vision, with satellite-resolution optics mounted at eight points on its head and tail, for maximal surveillance coverage. She was synched through a wireless neural interface that gave her direct input to the drone's systems. The link was a custom job that enabled her to use her threshold abilities to move her consciousness through the drone's onboard sensors as well as control its flight. Its wings were her wings. Its eyes were her eyes. By assuming the drone's phenomenology as her own in this way, she eliminated its response time to input so that it felt like her body, one she had made her own.

She had finished surveying the physical layout, activity patterns, and security of the corporate campus proper, including the greenspace where the sculpture garden was located. With Whit still out, she decided to fly a pass through the heavily protected Boeing-Marubeni executive residential compound on a lark. The Tombo was quick and light, but powering the high-res signal broadcast had drained its air time. She landed on the underside of a roof overhang to recharge. She accessed the local grid under a spoofed ID, and the drone began siphoning juice to fill its power cells. There was no drone there as far as the local secscan logs would show, just a strand of bubble lights from a holiday display. The Tombo could only pull as much power as the spoofed device ID would allow, and at the ampere permitted for bubble lights it was going to take a while to recharge.

As she waited, she pulled her mind out of the drone and scrubbed back through the vid footage on a hirez display in the truck cockpit, looking for one of the yards she saw on recon. At the same time, she pulled up her croquis program in her optical display. It opened with the last designs she had been playing with—a capsule collection of knitwear inspired by 2030s apocalypse culture and alpine motifs, modeled by chibi avatars of her itaku team. She took a moment to pose the team character mannequins in a festive caroling tableau and contemplated changing the edelweiss ribbon on the ghillie-suit lederhosen ensemble that chibi-Bob wore.

A notification from her research parasoft slid into view and caught her attention. The first item it had was the weekly report she'd set up that tracked novel vocabulary changes in 'trix flows and graphed their frequency distributions against image data tagged by specific blades of street fashion fandom. The second item contained a predictive supply chain analysis of a potential manufacturer for custom alloys. The last, however, was the background search she had set for Lambert Erskine. She snoozed the first two and opened the third.

She glanced at its data graphs, then skipped to the search summary. The parasoft had pulled a wealth of public legal and news records from 2064 to 2066. There was little before that period, mostly society mentions and auction records. The results trailed off to nothing by 2068. The parasoft had run into hardened nodes in its search, however. That definitely implied further results inaccessible to public searches. It asked her if she wanted to authorize autonomous escalation for the search. She frowned and sent it to her to-do queue instead. Going through the results more closely could wait, and there was no telling what hidden flags an autonomous escalation might raise in the wrong corners as it tried to go after the darkened data.

She returned her focus to her croquis program. Yes, the collection definitely needed some refinement before it would be ready to go into production for her Doom Princess Couture line. That could also wait until later. She logged it in her schedule as a task for next week, then opened her default mannequin, a marble statue of a young woman reaching out and looking up at her hands with an expression caught between a smile and shock. Sakura sketched a rough outline in the air, and with a flick of her fingertip it transformed into an untextured dress mesh. She carved some vertex adjustments and then flicked it onto the professor's model. In the recon vid, the stream hit the frames she had wanted. She paused playback and smiled, then brought up the swatch menu in the croquis program and started flipping through libraries of floral barkcloth.

The cabin motion detector alert woofed and flashed, and she shifted focus back to expand the interior camera feed. Whit's goggles had come out of sleep mode, and the lenses became semi-transparent from the outside. He opened his eyes and sat up, swinging his legs off the far seat. The mage stretched his neck, clearly working out a kink that had settled in while he had been out of his body.

"Not that it matters now," he huffed. "But I can't believe Billy's plan got more votes than mine." He leaned back and slung his arms over the back of the seat.

The Rover's internal log showed he had just accessed the visual feed from the Tombo. Sakura reset the drone footage playing over the commnet so he could access it timestamp-keyed to the infrastructure systems datamap she'd recorded in parallel. "Seriously? You come back from astral recon, and that's the first thing out of your mouth? Chummer, you need to let it go." She enunciated the last three words. "You know we needed a more subtle approach to get in and out, fast and no-friction. And, c'mon. Billy did vote for your downtown art scene LARP."

"Yeah, I'm a little worried about his newfound enthusiasm for the arts," said Whit. "'Gallery owner' was probably not the best cover for him to use on the public BoeMaru factory tour. I should've gone with them."

"He's got Bob with him, it'll be fine." The factory line Billy had insisted on visiting "for case omega recon" was on the other side of the Boeing-Marubeni complex from their target. She had been about to point this out, but then she figured out that the facility, which had been the largest building in the world until 2031, was also where the commercial helicopters were assembled. No wonder Billy had wanted to go.

"Sure. As long as no one mentions the animals in the avionic testing labs," he muttered. In a louder voice he said, "So I didn't see any major magical red fla—oh!" He scrambled up in his seat and flicked his goggle controls. The lenses turned dark as they played the recon vid in VR mode. "There—go back!"

Sakura scrubbed back the feed over the commnet as he waited. She had a feeling she knew what he had spotted.

"Stop there. Can you clean up the feed?"

She adjusted the light field's depth of focus and increased the contrast and detail as she zoomed in the view. A three-meter-long Boeing-Marubeni Cromwell aerial drone cruised a loop around the yard of one of the larger houses in the executive compound. It had been modified with an aft platform and a red light on its nose. A waving Santabot sat astride the front end of the domed fuselage like a Christmas cowboy, while behind it on the platform a pair of mechanical helpers exchanged kisses on top of a mound of wrapped presents. The Santabot wore a Hawaiian shirt and fur-trimmed hot pants; its helpers wore considerably less.

"I thought you would appreciate that."

"ADGMACH," Whit said. She had no idea what that meant in Enochian, but it sounded like agreement. "If Billy did have a gallery, that's the kind of art it would have."

"He'd make 'em take the sleeves off Santa's shirt first."

Whit sank back with a sigh. "The artist's eternal conflict

betwixt Muse and Mammon. I think we've found our theme for the lodge's solstice party."

"Our holiday party theme is 'making art or making bank?' That's…topical," she said dubiously. She hadn't expected him to take the abstract high-concept route. Billy might get into it, given his current method-acting kick. Taking the camp out of the holidays didn't sound much fun to her. It was what made them bearable, after all. That, and friends. And hilariously inappropriate gift exchanges.

"Uh, I was thinking 'Santa's Polynesian Workshop,'" Whit said, "but if you'd rather go with 'false narrative of maintaining creative integrity within an extractive capitalist structure that uses it as a mechanism to perpetuate economic dispari—"

"Nope!" She exhaled with relief. Solstice was saved. "'Inexplicably Hawaiian Santa' is good for me."

WEDNESDAY
19 DECEMBER, 2074

2 DAYS UNTIL WINTER SOLSTICE

CHAPTER 6

THE ORIGINAL ITAKU WIPED THE blood splatter and rat hair off his safety visor. It was like putting chrome on a monster truck as far as his own protection went, but he liked to model responsible decision-making for his comrade-workers. It let them know they were all in this struggle together. He wouldn't ask anything from them that he wasn't willing to undertake himself, especially something this messy and sensitive.

He looked at the shredded dire rat he held in his retracted grapple-gun hand. He hadn't realized he'd popped the rat after electrocuting it, but hot frak, was he fed up with these damned vermin. This was the second incursion in as many months, and the little buggers weren't falling for the no-kill traps that did the job last time. He needed to figure out how they were getting in, or there was going to be trouble. He was proud of The Flatline, as much of its profit-sharing plan as its collection of sci-fi memorabilia. But these didn't amount to jack if their users didn't have the reassuring comfort of clean, rat-free restrooms. Null spoof, right now his concern was for his customers and comrades. They deserved better than to share their johns with a bunch of bad-tempered rodents.

A fist banged on the bathroom door as he dropped the rat remains into the heavy black garbage bag at his side. The cyberlimb machine gun was out and pointed at the door before he realized he'd raised his right arm. "Uh, this unit is occupied, chummer." He tried to keep it light. *Don't let them know anything is wrong. Keep it together, cowboy.* "You should interface with the next one."

The Original Itaku surveyed the bathroom carnage around him and resigned himself to spending another afternoon doing a deep-clean. He sighed. He had been looking forward to personally delivering the badges he'd made for the BoeMaru job, getting to spend some quality time with his teammates off the clock, maybe swap some good itaku stories, but it wasn't meant to be. Today, The Flatline needed him.

CHAPTER 7

BILLY SAT ACROSS FROM WHIT in the back room of the safe house, where they were waiting for The Original Itaku's courier to deliver the badges he'd made. They'd get the team inside BoeMaru proper, beyond the tourist areas Billy and Bob had scouted. The target was in a standard issue corporate park, just a really big one, was what he'd gotten out of the recon briefing Whit and S2K had given them. At least he had finally gotten to see the plant where they made the Zephyrwolf line of helicopters. Someday he'd have one of his own. A ZW-221 Breeze, or even a ZW-990 Sirocco. Like Grandma says, "Patience makes a long road short."

In the meantime, Whit was teaching him how to play Tarocchino.

Whit shuffled a deck of tarot cards. "I usually play Ottocento, the one you play with partners. But we'll play a two-person version while you're picking up the basics." He dealt five cards to each of them. "If players don't like their hands, they can recall the cards and start again."

Billy looked at his cards. The cards all had pictures, some with detailed scenes. "No, these are cool."

Whit nodded, then dealt the rest of the cards quickly. "Okay, now you look at all your cards and figure out what combinations to declare if you want the extra points. They can be cards in sequence, or the same kind—like straights and flushes in poker."

Poker, right. That helped. Billy looked through his pile of cards. They didn't look anything like a poker hand. "Uh, I've got a skeleton, and a guy and girl making out?" He fanned them out. This made no sense. He fleetingly wondered if his lodge brother had started inventing rules to imaginary card games out of boredom. Unlikely, but it would make more sense than trying to put a poker hand together out of the cards he was holding. "Also some swords. And a guy hanging upside down. How am I supposed to make a straight out of a guy hanging upside down?" He narrowed his eyes at Whit. "Is this a real game?"

"Let me see."

He passed over his hand, and Whit began rearranging them methodically.

"Okay, these cards are called trumps. Most of them are worth one point, like this one." The mage pointed to the skeleton. He handed back the cards. "You could declare a suits sequence in swords if you want, but you don't have to."

A red light flashed above the door to the front room. Someone was outside on the street, ringing the storefront doorbell.

"Bet that's the courier," Whit said.

"I'll go," Billy said with relief. He jumped to his feet and ran to the door. He looked over his shoulder at Whit. "Don't peek at my cards while I'm gone!"

"But—"

Billy slipped out the door and closed it behind him before the mage could finish his sentence. Between the steel filaments in the outer safety glass door he could see a tall figure standing on the sidewalk, jabbing a finger at the doorbell button.

He vaulted over the empty counter and landed at the entrance. At the door stood an elf with blunt-cut fringe and hair spiked haphazardly in glittering black and fuchsia spears of varying lengths. More glitter was sprinkled across her dark cheeks like stardust freckles. The form-fitting biker leathers that she wore under the pink tutu had seen better days, but the AdTag patches scattered over their surface shone brightly with no dead zones. Most displayed standard syndicated revenue-paying content, while the remainder had been hacked to play Flatliner promos or body horror blipvids. She had a messenger bag slung high across her back and held a rumpled bioplastic bag with The Flatline's logo in the hand not assaulting the doorbell.

He recognized her as the bartender from The Original Itaku's theme bar. It had life-sized character models straight out of action vids from the last century. Vector matrix speedruns played on cheap wall displays, and there was chrome everywhere, lit by old-fashioned neon lights. You could feel the love The Orig had put into the place. It was awesome.

He opened the door. "Hi, EmPee! It's good to see you. How have you been?"

She acknowledged him with a dour twist of her mouth. "Oh, lookey. It's Billy," she said in a monotone. She put the bioplastic bag down on the sidewalk and unslung the messenger bag. Out of it she pulled out a thick, padded trimesh envelope, which she handed to him.

He reached out and took hold of the envelope, but she didn't let go.

"Do you, Billy, solemnly swear that you are Billy and not some rando slot pretending to be him, and that you are authorized by the dickmonkeys you work with to accept this package of a wholly non-criminal and flat-legit nature, on their behalf, or face unspeakable consequences of an unspecified nature?"

Even after working in SEAplex off and on for two years, he was still trying to wrangle how people got along here. The folks he met mostly came in one of two flavors: the polite ones who somehow forgot that they'd had a friendly conversation with you as soon as it ended; and the other, rarer ones who'd tell you to your face to frak off as soon as they met you. EmPee was one of those. Her unsentimental dislike of most everyone, including them, was sincere. She didn't worry about what they thought of her, and that bluntness was a gift he was grateful for.

He figured either path was a kind of safety valve for the frustrations of living where there was so much to be had, yet somehow not enough to go around. Everyone was on guard against everyone else's hungers, as well as their own—for money, status, love, survival. He could feel the tensions simmer. Sometimes the 'plex made him feel like he was locked in a barn full of lambs with a pack of hungry coydogs, except the lambs here were also coydogs.

"I sure am," he said. "All that stuff. Except for the dickmonkeys. Maybe the zoo has some? Bob might know. I could go, try to get permission from one if you want." He might appreciate the honesty of her hostility towards them, but that didn't mean he wouldn't parry when she used it as a weapon.

She rolled her eyes and released her hold on the envelope. "Whatever, I don't care. The boss made me promise to ask you that."

"That I work with dickmonkeys?"

"Nevermind, you big idiot. He loves you shitball frakkers, frak knows why." She sucked her teeth in disgust. "He may actually have said something about 'my solid chummers this' and 'sacred trust that.' Same frakkin' gist. There was probably one of his dumb lines, too." She dropped her voice an octave. "'Adversity is a Bloom filter for true chummers,' whatever the frak that means." Her voice rose back to its natural register. "I dunno. I stop listening when he goes full-metal commie."

"He's got a big heart. He can't help caring." It was as though The Orig had to let all that love out or be overwhelmed, and he'd sink and drown if he didn't. "Like a shark."

"Frak off." She picked up the bioplastic bag and handed it to him. "Here. Lunch courtesy of The Flatline."

"Sweet!" He took the bag and opened it. Savory aromas of soy burgers and nooch fries filled the air. "Thanks, EmPee. That was really thoughtful of you."

"I spit on it." She looked over his shoulder. "Is S2K around?"

"Nope, she'll be around later though if you want to wait."

"Hang with you losers? Null chance. What about Bob?"

"Nope, he's doing Bob stuff." Bob had locked himself away in his clinic to work on his secret projects. Billy never asked what they were. He figured a person had a right to privacy when on their own business. It'd be different if Bob were family, of course.

EmPee's face fell into a dissatisfied scowl. "I was gonna tell him this month's batch survived longer than the last one, but whatever." She grabbed her motorbike and swung a leg over the seat. The elf pulled the bike off its kickstand, then paused. "Oh, tell Whi— What's-his-face that the boss's hair still looks like crap even after using that gel he rec'ed. The one that smells like a troll's taint. The boss can't cop to it, but that's the truth." She backed up and hit the biometric release to start the electric motor. EmPee spun the throttle twice with her fingers on the brake lever, and black smoke erupted from the back wheel as a crackling shriek ripped through the air from a sound pressure transducer mounted under the tail. She stood on the pegs to bounce the bike parallel to the sidewalk, then gave him the finger before pulling a wheelie up the hill and riding out of sight.

Billy returned to the back room. Whit had pulled his goggles over his eyes and was making that crooked frown he did when thinking through a problem.

"EmPee says hi," he said. "She brought lunch. With extra spit."

Whit wrinkled his nose. "Charming."

"No, man. I think she's starting to take to us. Used to be she wouldn't have mentioned it. This time she even used our names!" he said. "More or less."

"Hn." Whit gestured in the air and flicked a finger repeatedly toward the display wall. It lit up with diagrams, photos, and a virtual model that looked scientific, not magical.

Billy set the bag and envelope down on the table and sat on the edge next to them. "What's that?"

Whit pushed the goggles up onto his forehead. "Tubular nanomeres. I made a bet with S2K that I probably can't win, but I might as well try anyway."

"Huh." He heard the alley door open. He turned around as Sakura walked in, carrying a large bundle. "Hey, S2K. Whit's teaching me Tarocchino."

Across from him, Whit tapped his comm and the display shut off.

Sakura did a double-take at the now-dark display. "Oh, really?" she said to Whit. The corners of her mouth rose in a fox's smile. "Tarocchino? Don't you play that on weekends?"

The mage looked away as a rosy glow sneaked across his cheeks, and delight broke over her face. "I knew it!" she said smugly. "Someone has an elf crush."

"It is not an 'elf crush!'"

"I haven't figured out where the synthcaf comes in." Billy said, coming to his rescue. S2K gave him a disappointed look, but it got a chuckle out of Whit. "I guess that part comes later."

"Think fast," she said as she threw the bundle at them. Whit's head snapped around in alarm, but Billy had already caught the bundle out of the air. He had expected it to be heavy but found to his surprise that it was light enough to balance easily in one hand. He tugged open the snaps that secured the cover flap to find a jumble of white coveralls inside.

"I picked those up at a janitorial supply outlet. Whit, they should work with the uniform designs I sent you, yeah?"

Whit leaned over the piles of tarot cards between them and reached in the bag to pull out a coverall. He rubbed the fabric between his fingers and snapped it between his hands, then examined the printed label inside the collar. His eyebrows raised slightly in surprise. "These are new. The fabric, I mean. It's a new flash-spun ballistic polymer."

"Yeah, but they were in the seconds bin, so they were cheap," she replied, taking a seat on the other table.

"Nice. I can preserve the impact resistance when I remod them into the new uniforms. I've already got a mental construct built based on your sketches. It shouldn't take long."

"I figured. Any sign of the badges yet?"

"Yeah, The Orig's delightful bar minion just dropped them off, along with lunch." Whit nodded toward the bag on the table. "There's plenty, if you're hungry."

Sakura put up a hand and shook her head. "No, no. I think I'll pass."

"EmPee told me she spit on it," Billy said.

"Ah, but did she tell you before or after you took a bite?" she asked with a knowing glint in her eye.

"Before!"

"Wow." Sakura cocked her head thoughtfully. "She's mellowing."

"Told you," Billy said to Whit. He looked back at Sakura. "I think The Orig's positive energy is helping her discover her true direction." He hoped so. It would be good for both their paths.

"Maybe. I wouldn't bet on it, but I've seen less likely things happen in this town." She pushed off the table. "Sorry I can't hang. I've got a couple of custom jobs to finish back at my place, plus I need to prep the fabs for deployment tomorrow. Catch you boys in the AM." She waved and left through the alley door.

"And it's off to the salt mines I go," Whit said. He scooped up the tarot cards and deftly shuffled them back into a stack, which he shoved into a pocket in his coat behind him. He grabbed the bundle and the coverall he had pulled out and moved down to the far end of the table to work.

"Hey, brother, on mine—" Billy began.

"I know, no sleeves." Whit grinned at him. "I'll put in enough ease so you can wear your vest on the inside, too."

"Thanks, man." Billy smiled, grateful that Whit understood what his vest meant to him. It wasn't just a magical artifact under a geas from Grandma. It was a lifestyle.

THURSDAY
20 DECEMBER, 2074

1 DAY UNTIL WINTER SOLSTICE

CHAPTER 8

THEY MADE GOOD TIME COMING from the safe house on the south side. Early-afternoon traffic on the seventy-kilometer drive up to Boeing-Maruben was relatively light by SEAplex standards, despite the upcoming holiday weekend. Whit had spent most of the trip goggled in to work on his quixotic nanomere textile research. Recreating the lightwell effect convincingly with magic required that he understand how it worked materially, in general terms at the very least. The company that made the fabric guarded its trade secret well, and it was enervating work to slog through technical sources to piece together what technologies were likely involved, most of which he still didn't really understand.

When he pulled off his goggles, they had reached Lynnwood, and soon after they entered Boeingville, the local nickname for the large swath of land controlled by the megacorp. It stretched along the coast northward to the naval station and east from SR 525 to Fourth Avenue West. Beyond Fourth Avenue were the casinos, chem bars, and other, less wholesome businesses run by the organized crime that thrived in the shadow of the military-industrial engineering giant.

They passed Paine Field Airport, and its miles of tarmac, then made a turn onto the Boeing Freeway. It separated the main corporate campus and executive enclaves further north from the more modest gated communities for the rank-and-file citizens and the high-rises for provisional contract staff to the south. The immense scale surrounded them in the material sprawl of building after building, gargantuan warehouses and hangers, industrial parks and office towers, corporate cyphers that bore names like 44-21 or 40-103, all marked under the Boeing-Marubeni aegis.

The Rover turned onto the access road that looped around the corporate campus district. The entrance designated for contract and visiting workers was ahead on their right.

"Showtime," Sakura said over the commnet. "I'm pinging the security system now. Fingers crossed that we're golden."

They drove up to the auxiliary entrance where a guard station controlled access to the lot. Pressure plates under them clanked as they came to a stop, and after a short pause a guard walked over to the safety glass wall facing the truck.

"Good afternoon," the guard said over the external intercom. "Your work access pre-authorization documents have checked out. We just need to complete the weapons scan and activate the access badges that were sent to you by courier for, ah …" Her eyes focused on a point in the clear wall to her left as she looked at an internally rendered screen they couldn't see. "Ms. Kloss, Mr. Williams, Mr. McGraw, and Mr. Fauntleroy." The guard pointed to a scanner on the outside of the booth.

Sakura got out, but left the Rover running as she scanned her spoofed badge. The terminal gave a cheerful beep and played a canned welcome message asking if she would like to download the *Welcome to Boeing-Marubeni!* orientation map and manual. She demurred and returned to the privacy of the sealed driver compartment while the other itakus climbed out of the passenger compartment and scanned their badges.

Bob had a scarf wrapped around his head, and he pointed to his face when the guard asked him to remove it. "Phototosis. Medical condition. Don't worry! Not communicable!" He waved and ducked his head in a friendly nod and darted back into the passenger compartment as soon as the scanner cleared his badge.

"What's phototosis?" asked Billy as the mage climbed over him to the rear seats.

"Nothing," Bob said. "I just made that up. Sounds good, though. Better than 'fuck off with that hidden camera, or I'll melt your brain and sell your lungs on the black market,' right?"

Whit grimaced behind Bob's back. "Certainly more succinct."

A message from The Original Itaku surprised them over their comms:

>**Null sweat, chummers! Set a data bomb in their node when I**

**spliced in spoofs for ur badges. Gonna blow all 2day's data
@2300**

Sakura laughed over the commnet. "Maybe we should start calling him The Fairy Godmother, instead."

A second message came in:

**>brb gotta unload deliveries its 2-4-1 ladies nite tell ur
friends!!!**

Bob grunted. "Hell, no."

The gate opened, and Sakura drove them into the large parking lot. "Hey, S2K?" Whit called out as they cruised for a parking place that fit recon data analysis predictions for optimal cover and quick escape.

"What's up?" she replied.

"'Mr. Fauntleroy?' Really?" he drawled. "That's a terrible covert identity."

"I know a worse one," she said in a dry voice.

He groaned. "I'm sorry I didn't pick an edgy professional name, like 'Billy' or 'Bob.'"

She cackled over the commnet while Billy looked between him and the steel barrier that sealed the driver compartment, obviously wondering what he was missing.

"You can a Billy, too, if you want," Billy said. "I don't mind."

"You can be a Whit if you want."

"Thanks, but that'd be hard to explain to Grandma. I should stay a Billy." Bob had been listening to their exchange with his mouth half-open in wonder. Billy looked over the seat behind them. "Did you want to be a Billy, too?"

"Or a Whit?" Whit said, in the spirit of solidarity.

"No!" Bob's brow furrow shot up in alarm. "One of either of you is enough."

Sakura found an empty spot in the Boeing-Marubeni auxiliary workforce lot on the end of a row and parked the Rover. She launched the Tombo drone and piped its video feed to the team's encrypted commnet.

"That's the charging bay for the trams and carts that Boeing-Marubeni Facilities uses. They don't allow contractor vehicles on-site outside of the parking and loading areas, so we're stuck using one of those if we don't want to walk."

The feed showed a yellow "Charging" message on the hood of one of the carts turn green to read "Use Permit: Oppai Maintenance Services."

"I had The Orig get inside their vehicle pool control node so we wouldn't have to lug our gear around on foot," she continued as she got out of the truck. She walked around to drop the tailgate. "It's keyed to our RFID passes, so no one else should be able to drive away with it while we're working. Apart from Boeing-Marubeni security overrides, obvs."

They unloaded the Rover and carried their equipment over to the waiting cart. It was an open-top utility model with two rows of side-facing seats in the small flatbed behind the front bench. Sakura slid into the driver's seat and the minidrone followed her. It came in close to the cart and hovered behind her as she adjusted the iridescent green *kogai kanzashi* that secured her hair in a practical chignon bun. Whit hung back and lit a cigarette.

Bob exhaled heavily as he climbed in next to her from the other side. "Goddamnit, Whit," he growled. He gestured impatiently at him and shouted, "We're on a schedule!"

Whit extended his middle finger on the hand holding the cigarette. "Fuck you, Bob." He pointed to a sign and slouched against the back of the Rover. "They don't allow smoking outside the parking lot. I'm doing my part to be inconspicuous."

"Uh-huh." Bob gave him a jaundiced smile, then stared at the jungle of mohawk regrowth he had teased above his head into an unruly coxcomb. "Inconspicuous. Right."

Sakura leaned over the cart's steering wheel and watched him trying to blow concentric smoke rings. She turned to Bob. "You have to admit, he looks just like the kind of art school drop-out who would clean shitty corporate art for minimum wage."

"Oh, yeah," Billy said from the back seat. He grinned at Whit. "I'd totally hire you."

They waited for him to finish his cigarette, and then Sakura backed the utility cart out of its bay. At the same time, she flew the Tombo ahead, high above them on point, and assigned it to picket duty to alert them of any security activity. They turned down a permaturf service path that snaked along the backside of the Boeing-Marubeni administrative zone's concrete buildings. The path branched, and they took the left-hand fork that descended to the greenspace hub where the Garden of Wisdom and the incomplete Baphomet awaited.

A small army of uniformed caterers was setting up for that evening's tradition-agnostic holiday party. They ferried boxes of linens and floral centerpieces to buffet tables under white tents at the greenspace's near end. A black moon bridge arched over a small retaining pond in its middle, leading to the sculpture garden at the far end. The Garden of Wisdom itself consisted of a half-dozen sculptures set in a semicircle at the far end of the oval. Dense plantings of rhododendrons, ferns, and caladiums around the art created a sense of lush seclusion.

Sakura parked the utility cart in a pull-off area masked by a hardy bamboo stand. Bob settled back in the front seat to monitor the local astral space while the rest of them unloaded the gear. Whit helped Billy carry several long, zip-tied bundles across the lawn, over the arched bridge, and down to their target.

The most recent addition to the open-air gallery, the Baphomet stood at the near end of the collection. The chimeric figure sat on a pedestal a meter high, pushing the sculpture's total height close to four meters. The luminous ivory marble glowed in the mid-afternoon, the polished surface reflecting the light from a glass torch that rose above the goat's head. Its ridged horns swept up and out in a span broader than a basal human's reach. Soft eyes with deep, horizontal pupils seemed to follow them with enigmatic bemusement as they crossed in front of it. A gold-leaf pentagram shone on its forehead, and a pair of feathered wings framed its muscular shoulders. The athletic body was bare-chested, but carved drapery fell in soft folds over its priapic lap, from which a caduceus coyly peeked. The shapely legs, crossed demurely at the ankles, ended in massive cloven hooves.

He and Billy were unrolling opaque white screens and sliding them on to three-meter-long poles when Sakura walked over. She held a large case in each hand, and hugged smaller cases under her arms. She dropped them, and they hit the dense grass with muffled thumps. He glanced across the lawn at Bob, then up at Sakura standing over him.

"Nice of Bob to lend you a hand," he said. The other mage looked in their direction. "Because threat watch is important! Much more important than schlepping," he finished quickly. Whit gave Bob a wave and a weak smile. Bob shook his head and turned his back to them. Whit stood up and nodded towards the stacked screens. "We miscounted on the panels, I think."

"Nah, that looks good to me. We'll need to set them up around the other statues, um—that one, that one, and that one over there." She pointed across the lawn to three statues near Baphomet: a marble bas relief of Leonardo da Vinci; a bronze Ronald Reagan wearing an exosuit; and an animated, mixed-media holoprojection tableau of Jesus Christ, Gautama Buddha, and Sri Ganesha sharing a vegetarian pizza with Carl Sagan.

Billy rubbed his neck and looked towards the statues she had indicated. "Change in plan, S2K?"

She shook her head. "No, just a slight mod I completed last night. It'll take a little more time and effort to set up, so I brought extra panels as cover. Plus, we stand out less if we don't look like we're focusing on a particular target." She picked up one of the smaller cases and handed it to Whit. "This has your cleaning supplies, to use as props." She gestured to the cases on the ground. "You can leave these here, though."

Whit's brows drew together in concern. They looked too big to contain only the fabricated breasts. "What are those for?" A thought occurred to him. "Wait, S2K. We can't blow it up."

"No, no. Nothing like that. Don't worry—the satanic Johnson federation will be jizzed about the result." Sakura gave him an impish smile. "Trust me. They'll wish they'd thought of it themselves."

They started hoisting the assembled panels around the Baphomet statue. Sakura popped the latch on one of the large cases to reveal ample, ivory breasts that matched the sculpture's warm marble. Billy and Whit paused to admire her handiwork. Billy reached out, but she swatted his hand away. "Hey, don't touch. You'll get dirt on them."

Whit leaned over and gave the fabricated breasts an appraising look. He was unsure what to say about the strangely alien vision, nestled disembodied as they were in the case's protective foam lining. It was unsettling. He cast about for a respectful interpretation that he hoped would be appropriate for pagan icon breast augmentation. "Very…fecund?"

Sakura opened another case and pulled out a spray can of cleaning solvent and a red-and-white-striped shop rag.

"Thanks," she said over her shoulder. "I was leaning towards a sportier profile, but the more I thought about it, the more an aggressively bodacious vibe felt on message. Like, 'Check your slide, motherfucker, for these are the tits of destiny!'" she intoned in a commanding voice. She side-eyed Billy as if daring him to laugh.

Billy clamped a hand over his mouth and turned away, his broad shoulders convulsing under his sleeveless coveralls.

"Seriously?" Sakura rolled her eyes and climbed up onto the statue's lap to prep the chest surface for installation.

He elbowed Billy. "Mock not the tits of destiny." Whit's own voice threatened to break into laughter as he pulled away. "Lest their vengeful creator goddess smite thee, and deny thee thy ritual fruitcake and sacramental eggnog at ye magickal lodge party."

"Oh, man, I love fruitcake, especially when it's got those little green cherries. Those are the best," Billy said as they walked away to set up screens around the other statues. "Why do they exist? How? It's a complete mystery. Eggnog is okay, I guess, but I tell you what. Green cherries? That's the real holiday magic."

Ten minutes later, Sakura's voice came over their secure commnet. "Hey, Billy? Could you take over threat watch? I need Bob to come over here to take a look at something."

"I'm closer," Whit said. "Is this a magic thing?"

"No." There was a wary edge in her voice. "You should stay put."

Bob possessed an unusually eclectic background for a mage. There was the medical training from his life before going itaku, of course, which was standard vet school stuff as far as Whit could tell. But Bob had furthered his education since then to include expertise in demolitions, psychology, and cyberware installation and programming. The cautious expression on Billy's face suggested the same idea had occurred to him.

"Sure thing, sister. On my way." Billy shot him a tight smile then loped across the lawn in Bob's direction. The ranger slid into the utility cart at the same time Bob left it and strode toward Sakura and the Baphomet. Whit shifted position and turned his back at an angle so he could see them out of the corner of his eye while he ran a cloth over Reagan's moon boot to maintain his cover. Bob crossed the distance more slowly than Billy, but when he reached the statue, Whit saw Sakura nod towards a section of the base on its back face.

"S2K, can you patch your optical feed through the commnet?"

The stream opened on his comm just as Bob was bending down to get a better look. All Whit could see was his body blocking the base.

"Well, that's more like it." Bob sounded relieved. "Situation normal." He move aside, and the vid feed revealed what it was inside the statue's base that had alarmed Sakura. There was a digital timer, counting down from 04:19:90. It was attached to a cylindrical detonator lodged in a hefty lump of neon yellow plastic explosive roughly the size of a cantaloupe. Whoever had planted the device had also been inspired to sculpt the putty into the rough shape of a fist extending its middle finger.

"Normal?"

"Attempted sabotage by an unknown mad bomber?" Bob chuckled. "I say that's normal per our usual luck."

"You don't seem worried about this, Bob." Whit wasn't sure how big a blast that much explosive would produce, but its intent was unmistakable.

"Pshaw." Bob was coming close to sounding downright cheerful, which unnerved Whit more than the explosive hand. "You can't smell it without getting right on top of it, but this is the banana-peach formulation of Hi-C5. It looks impressive, but it's the low-joule flavor. Pineapple-Mango Lavaburst, or Durian-Lychee Splash? Trouble. But this mix is safe enough you could give to your scout troop to play with."

Bob was definitely freaking him out now.

Sakura cut in as the vid feed view moved away from the cavity in the base. "Okay. Bob, give yourself some space and disarm the device as discretely as you can. Whit, move the other screens to make it look like he's doing normal maintenance. I'm going to continue the installation."

"Hey, I was watching astral, and that guy from the night club is here." Billy's voice was excited as it hit the comm channel. "Which seems weird."

"Weird is relative today. Which guy from the night club?" Whit was carrying an additional screen to hide Bob, who had sat down at da Vinci's feet to work on the rude yellow hand. A thought struck him about the individual Johnsons and the absurdity of the device. "Was it the guy with the beard?"

"No. Was he supposed to be here? I guess I missed that part, too."

"No. No, he wasn't. Just curious." He was glad Billy's sighting wasn't the Johnson from the Satanic Fellowship. In retrospect, he sympathized with the Sisyphean difficulty the guy faced in building the Satanic Johnson coalition. His earnestness had been kind of endearing. "So which guy did you see?"

"The orc who was yelling at the troll on the roof."

As he rearranged the screens to better shield Bob from view, Whit racked his memory for details of that night before they got to the meeting. He drew a blank until Billy mentioned the cape.

"Ohhh, him. Yeah, vaguely. And you recognized him in the astral?" Whit had walked past the man that night and didn't think he'd recognize him now, but Billy remembered details that he often didn't.

"Yeah, although I first spotted him walking by. Looked like he works here. Weird, hu—he's coming back this way."

"Watch him." Bob didn't look up as he sliced slivers of plastic explosive away with a ceramic scalpel to expose the rest of the detonator. "Coincidences only go so far."

Whit wasn't sure if Bob was talking to him or Billy, but he thought the ranger would appreciate backup. He picked up the case of cleaning supplies and walked around the screens just in time to see Billy jump out of the utility cart and dash down the path in the opposite direction they had arrived.

"Ahh, Billy?"

"Yeah, hang on," Billy replied, his breathing loud over the comm.

Whit jogged up to the cart as casually as he could and looked down the path Billy had taken. He had run beyond the near bend, and a cluster of bamboo blocked further view. Whit sat down in the cart to follow astrally, and with a thought he was out of his body and down the path. He saw Billy's aura surge toward another, slower-moving aura, which he assumed belonged to Mr. Mysterious Coincidence. Both auras suddenly paused, then Billy's leapt over his quarry. The second aura darted back the way they had come, then veered to the side. Billy's aura followed and dove in front of it again and again, cutting it off like a sheepdog until the second aura turned and moved quickly back toward where the cart was parked.

Whit pulled back into his body to see the orc burst out of the bend in the path and duck into the parking bower, panting hard, his face damp with perspiration. He tugged at the collar of his shirt and did a double-take at Whit sitting in the cart.

"Hi," Whit said. The man's eyes widened with surprise, then he pulled out a pendant hanging on a gold chain around his neck. Whit started to cast a stun spell when the man murmured a phrase and clapped the pendant forcefully. His hands made a loud crack as they met, and Mr. Mysterious Coincidence disappeared.

"Crud," Whit said. He weighed following him astrally versus checking in with the team, and decided it was wiser to report what he had observed over the comm channel. "He activated an inert spell before I could drop him. We'll have to track him astrally, or let him go."

"I can track him in meatspace, but it'll be faster if I had someone with me to monitor astral while I hunt on the ground." Billy came jogging around the bend in the path. He leaned against the side of the cart and his face relaxed and his eyelids lowered a fraction. After a short time, alertness snapped back into his expression and he raised his head. "He's not nearby. Not close enough for me to see in the astral, anyway."

"We need to make sure he hasn't left any more presents that could fuck us over," Bob said. "Not to mention any potential accomplices who may be active."

"We could take the cart for recon, you driving and me looking astrally for his aura. I know what it looks like now."

Billy shook his head and examined the area around them. "I need to go by foot, so I don't miss if he leaves any spoor."

"You'll move faster on your own, then. I'd slow you down if we have to stop every ten meters so I can scan the astral without tripping over my own feet." Whit assessed the shelter afforded by the parking pad. The sculpture garden was located in the public-facing part of the corporate campus. The landscape architects had probably intended for the tall bamboo to hide unsightly facilities equipment from VIP visitor view, but it also hid him from Boeing-Marubeni employees walking by on the pedestrian paths between buildings. "I can help search for him astrally from here, then come back to the material to check in over the comm."

Bob cut in. "Why don't you send your spirit to find the guy?"

Because M'pixl-tpff gets wiggy when they come anywhere near you and the sucking void that is your aura, and you know it. "No, too many distractions," he said instead, which was true enough.

"Oh, for Pete's sake." Bob huffed over the comm. "Give me a minute."

Whit exchanged a questioning glance with Billy.

"I don't want to let the guy get away. I'm heading after him,"

Billy said. He took off at a run.

Whit slouched back in the seat and closed his eyes, slipping out of his body and into the astral plane. He rose up until he could see Billy's aura without interference. Around them, clustered throughout the spaces where office buildings stood, small lights shifting slowly, each one an aura belonging to one of the thousands of people who worked inside. Down on the more sparsely populated ground, Billy's aura moved swiftly, then slowed and made small circles as if searching. It paused, then moved deeper into the complex away from Whit.

"I told you guys to wait."

He felt a presence behind him, and turned. Bob was there, his aura in projection, with a spirit hovering next to him. It had manifested as a giant eye, with myriad irises in a rainbow of colors that continuously roved around its surface. One of the irises stopped and focused on Whit. The spirit had a dozen other irises targeted on Bob, jittering. The rest of the eye was sheathed in translucent pewter-colored skin, complete with an upper and lower lid and long, silver eyelashes.

"Billy didn't want to lose the trail." Whit kept Bob's aura out of his direct view so it wouldn't make him queasy.

"Well, I summoned a spirit to help find the guy. You'll need to give it the target's description. Try to use small words and clear images. I don't think I pulled a smart one out of the old spirit grab bag, if you know what I mean."

Whit visualized the orc's aura. A green iris that had been focused on Bob shot over to focus on him instead. At least the spirit was paying attention. "Male orc, wearing a fine-gauge tan cotton crew-neck sweater vest with three horizontal white stripes, over a long-sleeved, blue cotton oxford cloth button-down shirt." A tawny brown iris swooped over the eye's surface to join the other two irises focused on him. "And navy slacks with double pleats, no cuffs, and a half break. The pants are probably a hemp-aramid blend. Or maybe a rayon-aramid blend. I'm not sure." The brown iris drifted slightly away from the others.

"Good grief," Bob said. His aura radiated incredulity.

"I didn't get a close look before he triggered the invisibility spell!"

"Most people would lead with hair color, height, age. Esoteric things like that," the other mage said drily.

"Oh, yeah." Whit remembered an important detail. "He was also wearing a spent spell token in which an invisibility spell had been set, in the form of a disk. On a gold-colored rope chain." The brown iris snapped back and jostled the other two irises. They pushed back, each jockeying for the closest position to him. Other, nearby irises drifted over as if investigating the activity, and after getting bumped around by the first three, joined the competition for the center spot.

Bob turned to the spirit. "Go find the person thus described, then come back here and show us where he is." The spirit blinked once, then shot out on a weaving path.

"I'm dropping back into the meatsuit to check in with Billy. I'll be back in a jiff," Whit said. When he opened his eyes, however, there were two BoeMaru security officers standing over the cart. They didn't look happy.

"Hi," he said with a cheerful smile.

"You're a deep sleeper."

"Yes, yes I am." He yawned and covered his mouth as a distraction while he examined their auras. Neither one was magical, though, not even a thresher. They felt suspicious, but not hostile. He wanted to keep it that way, and aspired to be the slacker art janitor that his cover said he was. "Too many late nights at the studio."

"Do you have a badge?" asked the other guard.

"Sure do." He nodded at each of them in turn. "Oh! Would you like to see it?"

The first guard gave him a shallow smile. "If it's not too much trouble."

He patted his jumpsuit in an hurried way, eventually fishing his badge out on a lanyard around his neck. "Ah! There it is." He offered it to them for inspection, keeping his thumb on the badge's biometric plate. The second guard pulled a handheld scanner off her tactical harness and scanned it.

"He checks out." She showed the display to the first guard, whose shallow smile relaxed into appeased neutrality.

"Thank you, Mr.—" Her eyes tracked across her augmentation glasses. "Fauntleroy. Does your supervisor know you're hiding back here taking a nap?"

"Yes, ma'am." Whit rolled his shoulders back. "I am on a union-mandated rest break." The Original Itaku would be so proud of him for exercising his worker's rights. He looked at his comm. "For another six minutes." He yawned again.

The first guard scoffed. "They must be working you hard."

He demurred with a shake of his head. "Oh, executive artifact custodian is just my day job. I'm really an artist."

"What kind of artist?" The second guard looked genuinely interested.

"Printmaker! I am a printmaker. Mostly intaglio, some woodcut. Large format." He silently thanked his past self for paying attention in his art history courses. He fleetingly worried he was overplaying his hand, but he couldn't resist plunging further in. "My last series was a meditation on the anomie of human interactions in a synthetic society."

"That sounds fascinating. Did you have to go to school for that?" asked the second guard. The first guard rolled her eyes but now was also listening.

"Yeah, for sure." He had actually majored in Magical Arts at Reed. The closest he'd come to art school was junior year when the Hermetic and the Art De/Colony theme communities were housed together in the Old Dorm Block. He sailed on regardless.

"Studio art degree from Northwest College of Art and Design."

"And you can make a living from that?"

The first guard snorted and gave a cynical laugh. "Of course not, or he wouldn't be cleaning gull crap off art in corporate parks." She turned to leave. "Four minutes, fifteen seconds left, by the way. Have a good day." The two guards walked away from the parking pad.

He looked astrally to confirm they had returned to their rounds, or wherever it was that security guards went when not accosting starving artists. Their auras were moving away steadily but without urgency, and he came back to check in with Billy.

"Hey, Billy. I'm back in meatspace. Bob summoned a spirit to help search. How's it going?"

"Help would be helpful? I picked up his trail easy at the start, but it got cold once he stopped freaking out. I did catch a glimpse of him astrally, heading toward one of the bigger buildings, but lost him in a crowd on the way over. You?"

"I didn't see any signs of him, but I did pretend to be an artist for the benefit of BoeMaru security."

"Nice! I missed that while scanning astral. Did you tell them my gallery was repping you?"

"No." Whit lowered his voice in affected sadness. "No gallery representation, for I was but a humble printmaker trapped in wageslavery, casting my work and fortune to the whims of the four winds, and any synthcaf shop that would hang it."

"The world just isn't ready for your artistic vision yet. Some day, brother. Some day," Billy said with sympathy.

Sakura interrupted over the comm. "Speaking of artistic vision, I'm about a third of the way done here. What's the deal in the astral?"

Whit filled them in on the details of Bob's summoning activity. "My location may not be as secure as I thought, so I don't want to risk any more projection. I can monitor locally though, and pass info between Bob and us."

"Ask him if he deactivated the device."

He rolled his eyes, but he had offered to coordinate. "What did you do on your last gig? Oh, I was the magical message bot," he muttered ruefully. He slid back into the astral, where Bob was waiting impatiently. The giant eye was pointed away from him. Whit turned around to see its gaze was fixed on a building not far from the visitor's parking lot.

"About time you got back. The spirit found our guy. I couldn't drop down to tell Billy because it's acting like it'll bolt if I do." As Bob said this, the irises tracking him began to shake frenetically.

"S2K wants to know the device status."

Bob gave a blasé wave of his wispy, astral hand. "It's fine. I deactivated the detonator and shoved our mad bomber's magnum opus in an empty case. More importantly, someone needs to get over to his location to confirm and control before the situation gets any more out of hand. We need to know if there's an accomplice or a second shoe about to drop."

Disquiet settled over Whit at the implication. He dropped back into the material plane and relayed the messages.

"Fraknuts, how he'd get past me? He must've doubled back. I'm on my way," Billy said

"I'll tell Bob to send the spirit to bird dog the guy, then we can take him down."

"Sounds good. I'll be in place in about a minute."

"I'm in position," Billy announced over the comm. "I got an astral visual on the spirit, which is awesome-looking by the way. It just went inside this building."

"According to the map, that one houses the accounts payable department," Sakura said. She hummed. "Don't mind me, just multi-tasking while this conductive epoxy cures."

"That would explain the sweater vest," Whit said.

"Hey!" Billy said with righteous indignation. "Vests are wiz."

"Can you tell if he's still invisible?"

"No ide—"

Bob unexpectedly cut in on the comm. "Frakking hell. I lost tabs on the guy. He must've gone through a ward in there, because the spirit just buggered off."

"So he won't be invisible anymore, right?" Billy said.

"Maybe." Bob grunted, and Whit could hear the grimace that went with it. "Don't get your hopes up. He could've been written into the ward as a passe-partout. Then the spell wouldn't have been affected, and we're still screwed."

"I'll keep an eye open over here on the astral in case he comes out. We may have to go in there on a gopher hunt."

"We should sell his ass to the organ-leggers after this, as payment for the trouble." Bob's threat wasn't idle. He'd spent over an hour after one job trying to fit half a comatose killthrill gang in the back of the Rover to sell on the side. Whit had raised an objection, but Sakura had shrugged it off philosophically. "At least this way they'll be doing someone some good, unlike the rest of their pals whose brains you melted," she had said at the time. And although the gangers had been trying to kill them, she did have a point.

"The professional thing to do would be turn this guy over to the Johnsons," Sakura said. "But frankly, I don't want the hassle. Not unless they pay us more for the extra work."

"And even then, trying to work out a secondary deal with multiple Js?" Whit whistled. "There's at least five different agendas in play there."

"Perfect. We can play them off each other," Bob said. "Auction him off to the highest bidder."

"Make sure they've paid out the rest of our original fee, first." Whit could imagine how the rival Johnsons would react to news of a saboteur, and he didn't want to be caught in the crossfire. Pitting them against each other was inviting disaster. "Before they kill each other over some random frakker."

"Can you imagine the static?" Sakura gasped, way too excited about the prospect. "We can keep that as a possibility and decide after we debrief him."

"Speaking of, I'm going to join Billy. He'll need help on stake out, and the sooner I can get inside that orc's head, the better," Bob said.

Bob soon appeared at the parking pad, and Whit slid out of the cart. He watched Bob roll out towards BoeMaru accounts payable. He briefly glanced in the astral but saw no signs of their fugitive before he headed back down to the garden to check on Sakura's progress.

The Baphomet had one new breast, and the image reminded him of the legend in which Amazon warriors would amputate their right breasts to facilitate drawing a bow. Sakura sat on the figure's lap, holding the other breast in one hand while she threaded a screw into a small plate of circuitry with the other.

"Hoi, what's that?" he asked.

"Anchor plate for the upgrade," she replied distractedly as she focused on her work. "It's wired through internally to the power source in the base."

"There's a power source in the base?" He didn't recall seeing one over her optical feed when Bob pulled out the bomb. "You don't mean the detonator, do you? Bob said he deactivated it."

"Yeah, no. I brought a power source with me. Glad I went with the smaller field coils. I was concerned about output, but a half-centimeter bigger wouldn't have fit. And it's not like it's supposed to kill anyone. Just teach them a lesson they won't forget."

"Grope not the tits of destiny?"

"You got it." She jerked her head up. "Oh, frak."

"You mean, 'Oh, frak he didn't deactivate it?'"

"No, I mean, 'Oh, frak, I just dug out the floor plans from the info dump The Orig sent earlier, and according to its file, that building where accounts payable is officed has two other exits not on the map.'"

"Only two more?" Bob started laughing, his voice raspy over the comm. "It's our lucky day."

"I flagged the file in the archive. There's one exit on the east and one on the backside."

"Not a problem. We'll let you know when we have him in hand."

"Back to janitoring with me, then. I'll pick up watch down here," Whit said.

"Janitor away." Sakura gestured vaguely with the breast in her hand. He wandered over to where da Vinci sat contemplating his flying machines in profile and pulled out the cloth. The landscape architect had framed the statue with olive trees on either side, and a tall hedge of bushy camellias behind. The camellias were in bloom, double blossoms erupting in scarlet against the dark wall of leaves. Whit made a show of inspecting the statue and dictating notes about its condition. His performance would convince a casual observer, but the empty pantomime was starting to bore him. He hoped Billy would grab the guy, and Bob would get the info they needed, sooner rather than later. The camellias were nice, though.

He felt a breeze at his back and turned, just in time to see a clump of bushes shudder. He snapped his sight to the astral, and lit up among the pale green glow of the shrubs and olive trees and grass was a familiar and very welcome aura. Less welcome was the invisibility spell that was still attached to it.

Whit considered his options. The guy wasn't magical, so he couldn't attack him on the astral. Unfortunately, he couldn't lob a stun at the guy if he couldn't see him on the material plane. Sakura needed to finish the project installation, and he didn't want to attract any attention from BoeMaru staff. Maybe he could wait until Sakura finished, or Billy and Bob came back empty-handed… No, Billy was tenacious when he was tracking, and Bob's hackles were up so he wouldn't leave his stake-out either without good cause.

The aura forced his hand when it moved deeper into the garden toward the pizza-sharing tableau, in the direction where the orc had first run when Billy took up the chase. Whit pulled out of the astral and scanned the area for a proxy target. Theoretically, he just needed a living terminus to channel the spell's energy. He didn't spot another person, or animal for that matter. The shrubbery was alive, though, and it didn't vibrate at the same sentience wavelength the spell was keyed to. Any creature above that wavelength, like a person, in physical range would draw off the spell's energy and take the brunt of the stun. He'd have to cast wide and heavy to ensure it covered the area where Mr. Mysterious Coincidence might be, but if no one were in the bushes the spell's force would dissipate more or less harmlessly.

Whit inhaled. He drew the spellform into his mind, then glanced into the astral to confirm the distance. He snapped back into the material plane and rapidly collapsed a sphere of concussive force onto the rhododendron nearest the position where he saw the man's aura. He heard the heavy thunk of a body hitting the ground. A second later, he heard a quieter thump of a much smaller mass. He looked around behind him, but the closest civilians he saw were across the pond, setting up for the party. He turned back and warily pushed through the bushes. The orc had fallen less than a meter from the target rhododendron. Whit congratulated himself on hitting his mark. He approached the unconscious man slowly, and nudged him with his toe. No response. He knelt down and laid two fingers on the man's neck. Still alive, pulse steady.

"Hey, I just dropped the guy. He's out cold, but you all might want to come back here," he said in a casual voice over the commnet channel.

"What! Where?" Sakura asked excitedly.

"Behind the pizza party. On the Sri Ganesha side."

"Nice one!" Billy said. He sounded sincere in his congratulations.

"Goddamnit," said Bob, with anger colored by exasperation. "On our way."

Whit pushed back to his feet. He pivoted when he heard footsteps behind him. On instinct he looked into the astral for the threat, but it was Sakura weaving her way through the bushes.

Dropping back, he waved towards the man on the ground with a flourish. "Ta da," he said proudly.

She looked down at the man and shook her head with a sidelong smirk. "And you thought this job was a waste of our talents."

"Hn." He rolled his head to one side. "Probably still true. I do feel like I owe the rhododendron an apology, though." She looked at him quizzically, and he explained his maneuver against the shrubbery.

She laughed with delight. "I think magical assault and battery of vegetation is a first for us." Her smile fell. He followed her eyes to a grey lump lying on the ground.

"Oh, dead squirrel. Don't show Bob," she said.

"What dead squirrel?" Bob asked in alarm over the comm.

He remembered the second thump.

"Amma," he swore and ran over to the animal. He sank to his knees and gingerly touched its side. It wasn't breathing, but the body was still warm.

"Um." Whit looked at Sakura. She shrugged and put up her hands. "Bob, how do you do CPR on a squirrel?"

"The usual. Start with chest compressions, but be careful with the pressure. Don't press more than a half-centimeter. The rhythm should be about twice what you'd use on a human." The former veterinarian paused. "So it's not dead? And it didn't respond to a heal spell?"

Whit froze. He hadn't thought to try. He'd never used a heal spell on an injured animal that small. Would it even work on a mostly dead squirrel? He glanced at it astrally. There was a very faint edge of an aura still there. Sakura stared at him wide-eyed with her hand over her mouth, though he wasn't sure if it were in horror or to stifle a laugh. Probably the latter. He tapped the mute on his mic and put his finger to lips. She nodded, understanding. He reached his hand out to the squirrel, his fingertips brushing the silver fur.

He closed his eyes and pulled the structure of the healing spellform into his mind. As he focused his empathy, he could sense a change in the astral under his hand, knowing without seeing the haze of golden light manifesting there. "GIGIPAH," he breathed, and with a push of will directed it to the squirrel's fading aura. He could feel the golden glow sink into its body as he opened his eyes. The squirrel twitched convulsively and he jerked his hand away, startled as it flipped itself into the air. As soon as the animal hit the ground, it dashed away to the safety of a far-away tree.

He sank back on his heels with a sigh of relief and unmuted his mic. "Uh, yeah. The heal spell worked fine. I just, ah, thought it would be useful to know squirrel CPR for future use. You know, just in case it comes up."

"Oh, well. Good," Bob said.

"I'm going to finish up." Sakura walked back towards the open lawn, and lightly punched him on the shoulder as she passed. "Give a shout if this guy wakes up, or if the squirrels come after you in retaliation."

Whit waited in the dense shrubbery until Bob returned. The other mage examined the orc, who was still unconscious. "Just how hard a stun did you throw at him?"

"Not cold-slab hard." *Although the squirrel might disagree.* He rubbed the back of his neck. "But he still had that invisibility spell up. I had to cast in a pretty wide diameter, so."

"Yeah, the thaumaturgic draw coefficient being inversely proportional in that situation. Not a criticism." Bob confiscated the man's comm and rifled through his pants pockets, emptying their contents onto the ground, then went to his neck and removed the BoeMaru personnel badge and the spent spell token. "You take any blowback?"

"No, I'm fine. Probably helped that I was pissed off about being too slow on the draw the first time. I'm surprised he's still down. Maybe I cast harder than I realized."

"Well, I got something to bring him around." Bob reached into one of his coverall pockets and pulled out plastic zip ties and a microjet injector. He cinched the man's ankles and wrists, then rolled up the man's left sleeve and pressed the injector to the inside of his arm. After a few seconds their captive's eyelids fluttered and opened. He groaned deeply and struggled to stand. Bound by the zip ties, he only got to his knees before falling over onto his side. He stared at Bob and Whit with wild eyes full of fear and anger. He inhaled deeply, and Whit could see his tusks had been filed down. It was a common practice among career corp orcs, but sneered at as an assimilationist concession by many of the orcs he knew who pulled itaku jobs or worked the itaku services underground. Bob leapt forward and slammed his hand over the man's mouth. Bob bowed his head in concentration and murmured something under his breath. Satisfied, he focused on the man on the ground.

"This is how our little talk is going to go. I'm going to ask you questions, and you're going to answer them. How you answer them will determine whether or not I knock you back out and sell your meat to the organ-leggers," Bob said.

The man blenched, then narrowed his eyes. He glanced at Whit, who met his gaze with frank openness.

"He's not lying. He really will do that," Whit said, with a curt nod. "And it won't be the first time. It's up to you, of course, but I'd suggest you tell the truth."

The man looked anxiously between Bob and Whit then nodded his head energetically. Bob removed his hand warily.

"You guys are itakus, aren't you? You work for the highest bidder, like in the tri-vids, right? I can pay you, just let me g—"

Bob clamped his hand back over the man's mouth. He looked over his shoulder at Whit. His face hidden from the man, Bob made an interested moue. Whit twitched a shoulder up in affirmative response. He hoped the orc had more yunies in his bank account than he was worth as parts.

Bob turned back to his captive. "I respect your enthusiasm, but it's little early for the negotiation stage. First things first: who are you?" He took his hand away. The man licked his lips and began.

"My name is Bryce Finicum. I'm a quality control engineer in the commercial transport systems division. I'm a Taurus. I... have a girlfriend! Who will call corp sec if I don't come home. My favorite color is yellow. I moderate, well, co-moderate a late Cold War-era coffee shop AU blade for the *Eternal Embrace* fandom. We have a plot on the matrix if you want to—" Bob's hand was back over his mouth.

"Nice to meet you, Bryce. You should know that I know that all of that was true, except the part about your girlfriend who will call corp sec on your missing ass. I know she won't, because you don't have a girlfriend."

The man sagged, then nodded in resignation. Bob took away his hand and held up a finger.

"First lie. Strike one. Next question: did you plant that bomb?"

Bryce nodded.

"Why?"

"That statue is a joke! It's a slap in the face to the orcs who have lived and worked in Marubeni corporate for decades. When everywhere else treated us like sub-human animals after Immanentization, they offered us their citizenship. It's not perfect, but we've had real opportunities with corps like them. But after the merger, company culture hit the skids. We started getting passed over for promotions, elves and basal clades like you taking credit for our work, people making pig jokes like we're not standing right there next to them."

"True," affirmed Bob.

"Yeah, okay, that sucks," Whit said. He peered at Bryce with curiosity. "But why take that out on the Baphomet?"

"I was on the Wisdom Garden committee, and we were finally going to get proper recognition for our achievements in science and technology. We won the final vote! And then management had the gall to unveil that! Some kind of frakking barnyard joke?" Bryce kicked the ground in frustration, his zip-tied ankles making him look like a beached mermaid.

"All true, from his perspective," Bob confirmed. Bryce looked at him in confusion.

"How do you know? Calling me out on my girlfriend, who *would* call corp sec if she existed, by the way, was even odds. But how—"

"Bob's a merlin. He cast a detect truth spell after he pinned you to the ground. So it doesn't matter how well you lie. If it's not the truth, he'll know," Whit said. Bryce swallowed reflexively and a hopeless look overcame his face.

"So you figured if you blew up the goat, they'd let you put up your little sculpture in its place," Bob reiterated.

"Pretty much, yeah," said Bryce.

"Who else was working with you?"

Wrinkles of uncertainty appeared in Bryce's forehead. "You mean on the committee? There's a rotating group, annual appointments are made by individual departments, but our quorum is—"

"I mean working with you on the bomb plot," Bob said, his mouth pulling into a frown.

"No one. That's all me." Bryce held his head up with a proud smile. "And I made the bomb myself." His smile faltered, and he cast his eyes downward and sighed. "No one else was really dedicated to seeing change through. Even Sheila lost interest in getting our statue up after we were barred from the club."

"Nice work on the explosive sculpting, by the way," Whit said. "An expressive homage to political street art by way of a Brutalist fauvism. Very compelling."

"Things that go boom generally are," Bob said drily. He nodded at Bryce. "Who's Sheila?"

"Oh! She's also on the Wisdom Garden committee. She manages the self-guided weapons intelligence division, and she was the first orc to get TSS clearance at the Everett campus, in fact! But we don't talk about her work much, my clearance is lower. Uh, much lower, but she tells the funniest cat stories. She has this one ginger—"

"Why were you two at the club? Were you working with a Johnson?" asked Whit. Bob squinted at him peevishly.

"What?"

"I wanted to hear the cat story."

Bryce looked between the two of them, hesitation in his eyes. Bob raised a hand in resignation and turned his attention back to the orc.

"Yeah, go on. Explain your being at the club," he said.

"Oh." Bryce studied the ground. His mouth twisted to one side. "We got a tip-off that a bunch of Satanists were meeting that night. We were going to go in, rough them up a little, then get them to demand the statue be taken down since they helped get it put up to begin with."

"False," Bob said, the warning plain in his voice. He held up two fingers. "Strike two."

Bryce rolled his head back and sighed. "Okay, okay. We did get a tip-off. We heard a bunch of Satanists were pissed off about the new statue, too, and were going to do something about it. We thought maybe we could work with them to get rid of it. We didn't realize those idiots were only upset because it didn't have boobs."

"Hey!" Whit interrupted Bryce. It was one thing for him to

0 1 0
1 2 8
1 0 1

make fun of the Johnsons for their fussy melodrama himself, but he wasn't going to take this attitude from a mundane normie wageslave. "A breast-less yang Baphomet fundamentally undermines its conceptual integrity from a Hermetic perspective. And it's misogynist."

Bryce stared at him open-mouthed. "Not having boobs is misogynist?"

"Oh, come on. It's a cynical capitulation to bushwa that demonizes or erases the female body in any context not meant as titillation."

"No pun intended." Bob pinched the bridge of his nose. "Moving on," he said sternly, resuming his interrogation. "Tip-off from who?"

"Alex Ho— It doesn't matter, does it? Someone else on the Garden committee just mentioned it in passing. They belong to the Satanic Church. Or is it the Church of Satan?" Bryce's forehead wrinkled in thought. "I get them confused."

"This person told you when and where the meeting was going to be?" Bob sounded suspicious, but he didn't call a third strike.

"No," Bryce said slowly. "Not as such."

"So how did you find that out?"

Bryce hemmed and hawed. "I, I'd rather not say."

"Tell me." Bob leaned forward with a menacing air. "Or I'll shove myself into your head and find it myself."

"No, I can't! I could be terminated. I'd lose my job, my housing, my BoeMaru citizenship. I'm a middle-aged orc who's barely made it into management. No one would hire me." He looked beyond Bob and pleaded with Whit. "Where would I go? Go live in the Warrens, like the animals they say we are?" A SEAplex-megacorp coalition had built the complex of high-rises as refugee housing post-Immanentization. They'd made no formal agreement to sustain the project long term, however, and it had fallen into anarchy and disrepair after its political usefulness had diminished.

Whit regarded the orc with sympathy. "That's better than the alternative." He looked at Bob, then back at Bryce with a meaningful raise of his eyebrows. "Besides, I've been to the Warrens. They're not that bad."

"Says the basal tourist," Bryce replied, scorn dripping from his voice.

Whit laughed. To be honest, his trips to the slum, with its ad hoc maze of skybridges, had been mostly work-related, but they'd become infrequent since the disappearance of Tabitha, a legendary fence and their contact in the Warrens. "Point taken."

"Enough." Bob set his jaw and growled through clenched teeth. His stare bore into Bryce's eyes.

"What the— Stop that!" Bryce shouted. His mouth gaped open in horror. "Get out of my head!"

Bob clamped his hand over the orc's mouth to muffle his cries. Whit shuddered and turned away. Bob's interrogation techniques were bloodless and he claimed they left no permanent damage.

That didn't keep them from appearing in Whit's nightmares. He started to walk back to the open lawn but stopped when Bob snapped at him.

"Stay. Someone needs to stand guard."

Whit clenched his jaw. He didn't want to watch, but Bob was right: they couldn't afford any more interruptions. He crossed his arms and stared back at the other mage with undisguised resentment.

Bob closed his eyes and his brow furrow deepened as he attacked his captive's mental defenses. "He tasked an undergrad co-op working as a data monkey to inject a listener. It pulled relevant factors based on known players, then he ran a contact chain analysis."

Bryce thrashed under Bob's hand, but the mage continued his mind probe, undeterred and indifferent. The effort of forcing his will on another was taking its toll on his body, however. Bob's breathing grew heavier and he panted with exertion.

"Then he had an intern hack into Eden's reservation node to confirm."

"Sneaky devil," Whit said, with a note of admiration. Identifying disposable assets, distributing operational tasks separately. Bryce had struck him as being lousy at corporate maneuvering, but that was resourceful work. "If he gets burned by BoeMaru, he should consider a new career in *himitsu no itaku*."

Bob suddenly sank back. He braced himself with both hands

and took a deep breath. "That's all I can get, for the moment." He blinked with fatigue, then refocused on Bryce. "I might not be able to get inside your head right now, but I can still tell if you're lying."

Bryce had pulled his knees up toward his chest and was staring into space with a blank expression. He murmured quietly, as if he were talking to himself. "He told Sheila someone sent him an anonymous tip. She suggested they bribe the club's manager. They were going to wire the yunies to her. She would get them access to the meeting."

"Would you look at that," Bob said. He smiled with lidded, tired eyes. "That was my next question." He leaned forward once more and whispered something in Bryce's ear.

"Leave the statue alone," Bryce said in a monotone.

Whit held his crossed arms tight against his body as he watched the orc with concern. "Is he okay?"

Bob shifted his weight and waved dismissively. "He's fine. Nothing twelve hours of sleep and an analgesic won't mend. Well," he paused. A thin rivulet of blood began to drip from his left nostril. He reached into a pocket for a cloth and wiped it away. "That and maybe some therapy, which he probably needed anyway." He looked over at Whit. "You didn't want to ask him anything else, did you?"

Whit shook his head slowly. "I was going to ask him about the cape the other night. Why pick that to wear, of all things, but it seems moot now."

"Oh, for Pete's sake." Bob rolled his eyes. "Hey S2K?"

"Listening," she replied over the comm. "So, briefing takeaway sounds like wrong place, wrong guy, not a direct threat to the job."

"Affirmative. I dropped a subliminal direction not to mess with the statue anymore, just in case."

"Good. I worked too hard on these for some random corpmonkey to mess them up."

Bob pushed himself off the ground and stood, brushing leaves from the legs of his coveralls. He clapped his hands and rubbed them together with a smile. "So! Who's in for auctioning him off to the highest-bidding Johnson?" Bob asked, his voice hopeful and expectant.

Whit remembered Bryce's initial proposition. "I'm all for taking the guy up on his offer to pay us off."

Bob scoffed and looked down at the orc, who was curled up on his side. "I doubt that offer is on the table anymore."

"You don't know that." Whit pushed back. "He'll probably think it's a fair bargain if we promise not to rat him out to corp sec." Or to Sheila, for that matter. He had a feeling she would not be favorably impressed by her colleague's initiative.

"Regardless, he's not really in any condition to bargain now. I still say letting the Johnsons fight over him is our best solution here." Bob walked over to Whit. "You should contact your guy to set up the auction."

"No." He might have been willing to make the call to Alcime

if Bryce had been part of a conspiracy orchestrated by any of the Johnsons. But not for this.

Bob exhaled, exasperated. "Then give me his contact ID, and I'll do it."

Whit hummed. "Can't. I lost it."

Sakura snickered over the comm.

Bob stared at him with a flat expression. "You lost it."

Whit closed his eyes and nodded with a beatific smile.

"Look, Bob. The Orig can probably get you contact IDs for most of those chumps," Sakura said.

"Didn't you lose The Orig's contact ID?" Whit asked innocently.

"This is business," Bob fumed. He ran his hands through his thinning hair in frustration. "If you hate making money so much, why are you an itaku?"

"I don't hate making money. I just think the guy had a valid grievance. Orcs deserve better representation, and picking Baphomet seems pretty random in comparison."

"Fine! That's not a disqualification for turning him over. It's his fault for not hiring us to take his job instead."

"Rendition of agent provocateurs wasn't in the original deal. There's no reason to think the Js would bite at an auction offer."

Bob held up his hands as if to forestall the objection. "Don't worry about that. I can keep him in a medical coma at my place until we work out the details."

"No. It exposes us to way too much unnecessary risk," Whit

said.

"It could compromise our exit strategy," Sakura said. "We didn't pack for a ground-zero corp extraction. We'd have to ad lib it, and you know how that usually goes." She paused. "We do have those extra panels, though. We could break them down and smuggle him out like a big orc burrito."

Billy broke his watchful radio silence. "A burrito sounds good. After chasing that guy down? Twice? I'm starving. We should ditch him and go eat as soon as S2K is done."

"He's a bigger risk if we let him go," Bob said with an air of finality. He turned away from him and took a step toward Bryce.

"Not if we have leverage over him." Whit wasn't going to let Bob's ghoulish entrepreneurial side win today. He played what he hoped was his trump card. "Look, we know his plan, his associates, and more importantly, what he values and what he fears. And he knows that we know. Saying anything about this will make him the nail that sticks out. For corp nobodies, there's only one way that ends."

"And, he might hire us later to install his statue if we let him go," Billy said. "Double dip!"

"See? Letting him go is good business." Whit had doubts that Bryce could afford to hire them later, which would involve a much greater sum than his ransom, but the spell token he had been carrying would not have been inexpensive. Maybe transportation systems engineers made more than he realized. "On parole, obviously, with us as the stick and the carrot."

"I'm digging the biz dev angle," Sakura said. "We could use some more Johnsons on the ground. Ours don't seem to last long enough to make for much repeat business."

"He's a long shot and unreliable," Bob said curtly.

"Sure, but they all are. We can have The Orig tap his matrix and comm traffic. If he gets wiggy we can geek him then and drain his accounts. No auction fun or style points, but Bob still gets his parts money."

"Seems fair," Billy said. "I could still go for a burrito."

"And you still go home with three kilos of free explosive that you didn't have this morning," Whit said to Bob, trying to be conciliatory.

"Closer to five," Bob muttered. His jaw clenched once, twice, then he shook his head. "Fine, majority rules. We leave the mad bomber to screw us over for another day. We're knocking him out when we take off, though."

Whit walked over to Bryce. The orc was still lying on the ground with a glassy expression. "I don't want to hit him with another stun. He's still dazed from the one I threw at him earlier."

"I've got this. You can go." Bob grunted and moved to kneel by Bryce's side. "I brought some aerosolized moose tranquilizer that'll do the job." He patted through his pockets methodically, and eventually pulled out a small canister and a single-use, collapsible bag valve mask. He also laid out his scalpel and put it within arm's reach. Whit opened his mouth to object, but Bob held up a hand.

"There's a small chance of seizure or muscle spasm from the tranq. I'll cut the ties when it's clear he won't hurt himself from any side effects."

"Maybe explain our generosity as stone-cold professionals beforehand," Sakura said. "So he appreciates where he stands in this arrangement."

"I will impress upon him the unlikely good fortune he had in running across us today," Bob replied. "And the many benefits that will reward his good behavior."

Whit left Bob to his work and slipped out of the dark thicket of shrubs. He returned to the open lawn, trying to focus on how close they were to wrapping up, and not how he had passed up the ideal cover for a smoke break.

"I'm about done here. How's it look on the biz dev side, Bob?"

"All quiet on the upstairs and downstairs, S2K. Target is sleeping like a baby." The older mage sounded almost disappointed.

"Copy that, Bob" Sakura said.

Whit looked into the astral and saw nothing unusual. "All clear over on this side of the park."

Billy was leaning against da Vinci's feet and nodded at him. He picked up the remaining cases and handed one to Whit. "I'm thinking we should leave the screens up."

"Yeah, leave the panels. The longer it takes them to notice, the better."

Sakura was smiling at her handiwork as they walked up, cases swinging in hand. She climbed down from the Baphomet's lap and patted the now-buxom creature affectionately on the knee.

"The anti-grope system I added glitched out and took longer to de-bug than I expected. The final diagnostic panel is almost done running, so far so good." She stepped back. Swiping occasionally in the air, she watched the results in her optical display with an intent expression. She eventually nodded and gestured at the statue's chest. "How they look?"

Whit dropped the case and came closer. He folded his arms and pursed his lips as he rested his chin in one hand. Beautifully positioned and proportional to the figure, the breasts were indistinguishable from the original surface. He peered closely but couldn't discern any seams. Even the weathering blended. But then, obsessive attention to detail was a hallmark of Sakura's work. After a moment he spread out his hands in the air in front of him and grinned. "Paradoxically approachable, yet intimidating."

Sakura looked satisfied. "Excellent. Let's book it." She grabbed her empty cases and handed them to him, then picked up the large case he had ben carrying. "I'll take Bob's Hi-C5. He'll be mad if we leave it behind."

Bob interjected over the comm. "Damn right. Malleable

demolitions don't grow on trees, you know!"

They walked out from behind the white panels that screened the statue from ground level. Catering staff in black smocks bustled on the other side of the pond as they prepared for that evening's corporate party. They had already finished setting up the tower heaters and tables. He watched them laying out food and stocking bar stations, and realized he was a little hungry, too.

The itakus walked up the grassy incline to the parking pad and saw Bob waiting in the cart. Another utility cart was parked next to theirs, with an unattended rack of hors d'oeuvre trays in the back. Whit perused the selection and palmed a couple of savory tarts before climbing into the back of their cart with Billy.

"The art world is a lot more hands-on than I expected," Billy said as they drove off down the permaturf service path to the parking lot. "I'm not complaining. I thought there'd be more wine and cheese, though."

"Retirement goals?" asked Whit from the other rear seat. He passed the second tart over.

"Nah," Billy said, after some consideration. He took a bite out of the pastry. "The clients are high-maintenance, and art critics are brutal." He chewed thoughtfully for a moment, then frowned. "This pie tastes weird."

Whit brushed crumbs off the front of his coveralls. "I think they used artificial uni in the custard. It never tastes right, I don't know why people bother."

Bob glanced askance over his shoulder at Billy. "You do know we weren't running the art gallery LARP as cover for this job, right?"

"Well, you sure weren't." Billy shook his head and looked across at Whit with a long-suffering expression. "I don't know how he expects to work in anyone's gallery with an attitude like that. No wonder we didn't make any sales when we were on the factory tour."

Whit laughed.

Bob redirected his glare to Whit. He tried not to antagonize Bob further, but suppressing his laughter only turned it to giggles.

"I blame you," Bob said.

"Blame me?" he said, caught between embarrassment and gasping for air. "I was one-hundred-percent committed to the park janitorial crew cover, or whatever. You—"

A percussive sound wave blasted through the air above them and shook the utility cart. Sakura swore under her breath and flew the Tombo in a sharp arc over them, where it could get a direct view of the exit gate.

Billy was scanning the sky for signs. "That could've been a shock wave from a plane. It probably happens all the time around here. This may be totally normal." A sudden wail of sirens cut through the air. "Or, maybe not."

Vehicles swarmed into the auxiliary visitors' lot from roads coming in all directions inside the compound as they approached. Some were marked as Boeing-Marubeni security. There was also an unmarked van with a top-mounted sensor rig that screamed "rolling surveillance" as well as a couple of private subscription paramedic responder trucks. The utility cart slowed as they pulled into a charging bay at the near end of the parking lot. The Rover was two rows away from them. Nothing impeded their way to it, but the knot of security vehicles partially blocked the exit gate. Getting to the Rover would be easy. Making it out of the parking lot, on the other hand, was shaping up to be trouble.

"I don't like it," Bob said. A muscle under his left eye twitched.

"You don't like anything," Whit observed. Bob shook his head in irritation.

"That's not it. It's high-risk as an exit stage. We're going to be too exposed. Too many possible witnesses. Even if the hacker's paying attention, and doesn't have his head up his dick, and has reliable intel, and his access doesn't get cut off, and we manage to cruise out of here without getting shot in the face, we'd still be pulling too much attention. We can't leave without being noticed."

The risk of being noticed hadn't seemed to bother Bob much before, when he'd been riding high on the prospect of adding a warm body to the haul. Whit narrowed his eyes but refrained from saying anything aloud. Bob's moods were volatile at the best of times, and this wasn't one of those.

"Eh," Sakura said. "It's not like we've killed anyone today, or have a load of bodies in the truck for the organ-leggers, this time at least. We're just a normal work crew wrapping up a routine maintenance job. That's free invisibility right there. No one notices the proles."

Bob had already closed his eyes in concentration and begun to mumble. Whit looked into the astral, where a large fire elemental appeared. The column spiraled and pulsed with hostility. Tendrils of flame whipped out around them as it resisted Bob's summoning. With the roar of a hundred forest fires, the powerful spirit broke free from his control and escaped to its home plane. Whit returned his gaze to the material plane to see Bob sway on his feet and swear.

Bob opened his eyes, his face ashen with exhaustion. He grimly wiped away the perspiration that had started to bead on his forehead. "There goes Plan B."

Billy caught the mage by the shoulder when he swayed again. "Hey, man, we don't need to burn our way through. Null sweat. Whit and I'll get this stuff loaded into the Rover. Like regular working Joes would."

"Watch me," Whit said. "A regular Joe to the core." He grabbed an empty hardware case off the cart and swung it over his shoulder.

"Hoi hoi hoi, chummers!" The Original Itaku's voice broke in over the commnet. "Official channels say it was a gas leak, but the savvy-savvy says it's a magic bomb or somethin'. It went off a little ways from the southern edge of Boeingville, made a frakkin' sinkhole out of a city block. It's got the corps on burning edge, thinkin' it's a vanguard false flag staged by some itakus on a job. That, uh ..." He cleared his throat uncomfortably. "That wasn't you guys, right? You'd tell me if it was, yeah?"

"No, it wasn't us." Whit rolled his eyes. "We're not actually responsible for everything that blows up in this metroplex. Sheesh."

Billy shrugged but said nothing.

"Chummer, that's music to my ears. The HimitsuLink chatter is getting fractal up there, the street mages are loosing all chill."

"Is BoeMaru locking down? I'm not leaving the Rover here," Sakura said.

"Negatory on the full lockdown as of yet, chummer-chan," The Original Itaku replied. "Anticipatory protocols have been triggered in the manufacturing, design, and testing pools. Null sweat, that's all SOP under a category-three incident report. There's an advisory alert, but no restrictions yet on the civilian areas. I'm in the perimeter control layer, keeping your pass green. You should be able to motor out null glitch."

The itakus looked at each other, then at the security activity growing around the gate. They finished unloading the cart and carried the cases to the truck. Sakura popped the tailgate.

Bob scowled at the armed personnel milling around the vehicles. "I still don't like it."

"I got the Tombo up there on surveillance, but I don't think I can get anything with more range or firepower up in the air to cover for us without them noticing first," Sakura said. Her face stilled for a second, then her eyes widened. "Oh! Strike that. I do have something. Sorry, Billy. This was supposed to be your Christmas present." Her manic smile belied the rueful tone of her voice.

"Happy to contribute to the greater good," he replied with an affable shrug. "Wait—" His face froze. "Is it a helicopter? Were you getting me a helicopter? Holyfraknuts! You're…you're not blowing up my helicopter. Are you?"

"Ahh, nope. No helicopter for you this year. I'd keep writing those letters to Santa." Sakura's gaze unfocused as she started to work over her data link. She waved them on as she walked past them. "Go ahead and load up. This will just take…a couple… minutes."

Whit and Billy sat in the passenger compartment of the Rover and did their best to look like bored workers while subtly watching for any changes in the Boeing-Marubeni security presence or in the astral plane around them.

Bob was hiding under a tarp in the rear cargo area behind them. "No witnesses, damn it, no witnesses," he muttered to himself.

Sakura came trotting back to the truck from the direction of the security hut. Behind her, an SUV with Boeing-Marubeni decals backed out of the exit lane it had been blocking and parked in one of the Accessible spaces nearby, clearing their way to the perimeter road.

"We're good. Looks like we miraculously found a hacker who's on the ball," she said as she pulled out a trimesh Faraday bag from a pocket in her coveralls. "Here, put your passes in this as soon as we're through the checkpoint and on the road." She opened the driver's door and slid inside. "I've still got that exit diversion in play, just in case. Buckle up, we're heading home," she said over the Rover's closed commnet.

The Rover rolled up to the security hut.

Whit held his breath and watched in his peripheral vision for any reactions from the security personnel surrounding them. The guard inside smiled and waved them through, and the caltrop plate retracted and the baffled high-impact gate trundled open. The SUV that had been blocking the exit pulled up behind them as Rover drove past the guard house and through the perimeter barrier, but it was resuming its blockade position, and no one followed them out. Still, he didn't relax his guard until they crossed over the commuter rail tracks at the far end of the Boeing-Marubeni complex, with the open highway in sight ahead of them.

They were heading east on the Boeing Freeway when they noticed a low-flying drone with a red light on its nose closing on an erratic path behind them.

"S2K." Bob sat up in the backseat to look out the rear window. "Incoming."

"Don't mess with it! That's the exit diversion," she said over the commnet. "And also Billy's Christmas present."

"Hoi, you guys, check out Santa!" Billy tried to roll down his window to get a better look at the hijacked drone, with no success.

Sakura messaged Whit:

>**Try to keep him from highway surfing if u can**

He heard the chime of the window controls releasing for the passenger compartment and grinned. "Look out for riptides," he said to Billy, who was already halfway out the now-open window.

The drone and its crew of jolly elves passed overhead, veering north toward the main Boeing-Marubeni corporate campus. Billy was sitting on the sill and gave one last wave to Santa's receding back before he swung himself inside the car with one arm. Bob stared past them, following the drone's path and shaking his head. He balled up the tarp under which he'd been hiding.

"Bah, humbug."

Whit mulled over The Orig's intel report as the Rover sped along the freeway towards I-5, which would take them southwest and back to Seattle proper. He couldn't think of any targets in the coastal Snohomish 'burbs big enough to merit a high-wattage itaku squad. A Mafia family ran casinos in the town, but those were an open secret and, like the other obvious sites, they hadn't been hit. Maybe the magical disturbance had been a diversion for a deep-cover op on the megacorp compound, after all. Or cover for something going down quietly at the naval shipyards north of the main campus. 'Burbite culture mystified him, but the blast seemed like overkill for a wageslave upset about their neighbor's yew growing too far over the property line.

"Hey, S2K? We're taking I-5 all the way back, right?" Whit asked.

"I figured we would. Problem?" Sakura replied over the commnet.

"Nope. Hey, can we stop off for synthcaf on the way back? I'll buy for everyone."

Sakura laughed. "No, we are not stopping so you can smoke."

"That was not my motivation." Billy was watching him drum his fingers urgently on the seat, and at this shot him a doubtful look. Whit slid his hand under his leg. "I'm curious about the blast. Aren't you?"

"Not really." The Rover took a right onto the highway on-ramp to the pass-restricted elevated track. They passed under the first of two steel arches that controlled access to the expensive, but less congested roadway. The light curtain the arch projected faded from a pulsing orange to a faint green, and the message on the signature holosign ahead changed from traffic conditions to read, "Welcome [('$veh', 'pass("An unknown er..")] to the Expedited I-5 Travel Experience, Brought to You Today by: Smoke 'N' Choke Comfort Plazas." The grid of red laser beams that cut across the inside of the second arch twenty meters beyond deactivated.

"Things blow up in the metroplex all the time," Billy said. "I figured that sort of thing was normal here."

"Et tu, Billy?" So much for solidarity between lodge brothers. Whit whipped around in his seat to appeal to Bob in a last-ditch effort. The irritable mage would probably shoot it down, too, but it was worth a try. "You want to check it out, though. Right?"

Bob had made space on the floor in the rear to lie down with the rolled-up tarp as a bolster for his back. He lifted his head to consider Whit's question and pursed his mouth in thought. His brow furrow twitched. "I am a little curious."

"Now that I think about it," Billy said slowly in a loud voice. "I just remembered how hungry I am. We should stop for that burrito." He caught Whit's eye and winked broadly at him. Whit smiled back at him in gratitude.

"Frakking merlins are a bad influence," Sakura said, but there was little rancor in it. "Yeah, okay. But the traffic map shows massive lag down on the free level, even more than usual for that stretch. We can try for a drive-by, but no promises. And no stopping!"

They passed the I-405 interchange, and traffic on the highway's upper toll level started to slow as well. The next highway holosign read "ALERT: I-5 Security controls enacted for your protection. All exits closed next 5 miles."

"Hey," Sakura announced. "If you want to take a look, this is as close as we're going to get. I don't think it's worth wasting time doubling back or risking checkpoints on surface streets if they're still on high alert."

They were still a fair distance from the blast site. He couldn't take the risk of astrally projecting from a moving vehicle, but he could still scope out the site, albeit with a more limited range. The fine hairs on the back of his neck stood up as he looked into the astral. He didn't see any anomalies, but he felt them. He hadn't expected to sense disturbances to the ambient mana flow from this far away. The sensation intensified, and he shivered involuntarily as they drew closer, driving down the section of road where the exits had been shut down. The sensation gradually resolved into visible details. A translucent gold dome shimmered against the grey astral sky and enclosed the site to the west. Jagged arcs of silver and black energy shot out sporadically from a point within, and they flashed white when they hit the ethereal barrier. Faint lavender waves of energy rippled through the dome and dispersed well beyond its confines, so it wasn't just a containment barrier. He wondered what was generating the waves. It could be residual disturbance, like those erratic discharges, if the initial blast were intense enough to change the mana differential inside the dome. But it could also be a diffusion current caused by ley filtering, which meant the mana contained inside the barrier had been tainted or disordered by whatever had happened.

The accident had attracted a crowd. He was too far away to discern individual auras, but he could see glowing clumps of light milling around the barrier. Probably a mix of SEAplex civil responders, private first-responders on subscriber calls, and random locals out to gawk. He doubted there were many blast survivors among the massed auras, given the magnitude of the residual disturbances. Hanging back from the site, far above the ground, was a scattered star field of magically active auras. They streaked in and out, probably mages projecting in from elsewhere in the metroplex to rubberneck.

The Rover was south of the site now, and the details were fading from view. The hairs on his nape relaxed. He slid out of the astral and noted their location, to gauge the affected area's size. He might be able to calculate how much power had been released and narrow down possible sources by inference later, just for fun.

"Hey, Bob…"

"Yeah, I took a gander at it. Maybe a mile away, to the west there. Hard to tell what could have caused it, but it sure as hell wasn't mundane. Massive mana bomb, or a ritual spell triggering… can't say. Ambient mana disruption was high, and that ley filter would've destroyed any key signatures."

"Kinda weird they had a ley filter set up so fast, outside of the Elflands."

"Don't know about the Elflands." Bob grunted without commitment. "It wouldn't shock me if a high-sec neighborhood in town had access to one, or the big corporate research enclaves. But out here in the open 'burbs? Sure, that's a little odd."

Whit leaned his head against the window. He made sure the

anonymizer agent was running on his comm, then sent it outside the Rover's closed commnet to hit up HimitsuLink. The main scroll was spinning with "hotshot itaku disaster" rumors. If any of them were true, that job existed so far above their own pay grade that it might as well have been on another plane. He felt depressed and mollified in equal parts that even elite itakus had to take crappy 'burb jobs on occasion.

Traffic into the city center remained slow as the day creeped towards early evening and the winter sun started its descent into night. He shut down the HimitsuLink connection to watch the dying sunset bathe the suburban landscape with diffuse pink and orange tones. The greener, more open development at the north end of the city eventually gave way to dense outgrowths of looming glass and steel, and the ambient urban glow supplanted natural light. Bright billboards competed with one another on the sides of microcorp buildings, their animated loops reflecting off near-by windows and sheer polished walls to beat out an silent rhythm of color and darkness that intensified the deeper they drove into the metroplex.

As he drifted off to nap, the muscles in his shoulders and back relaxed. Whatever had gone down in the northern 'burb, it was someone else's mess to clean up. They pulled off their own job with only a small hitch. The remainder of their payment would be waiting for them to pick up later that night at the agreed-upon dead drop in town, and his share would be enough to not sweat hustling for jobs for a month, at least. Not enough to take the winter off, but that was fine. As The Orig had proclaimed at the start of his first job with them, "Rest keeps a chummer sharp, but too much downtime blunts even the best razorgirl's edge."

FRIDAY
21 December, 2074

Winter Solstice

CHAPTER 9

WHIT HAD FALLEN ASLEEP ALMOST as soon as he'd gotten home after the uneventful payment pickup. He woke up the morning of the solstice to the murmur of slow thunder as a distant storm passed. It came close enough to drop a light rain on the roof, the sound dampened by its reclaimed rubber shakes. He rolled out of bed to make a carafe of synthcaf. He preferred to measure out components by hand, but feeling groggy he picked a preset blend instead, a restorative light on the methylxanthines and heavy on lysine and B vitamins. It was worth enduring the wet cold outside for a smoke on the stoop while it brewed. A narrow overhang partially sheltered the front door, but it did little to block the mist blown by the wind. Eventually discomfort won out, and he retreated inside. The synthcaf had finished brewing, though, and he crawled back under the pseudodown duvet with a full mug.

Emotional malaise and mental exhaustion always hit him to some extent after a job, no matter how much sleep he got, and the nootropics hadn't yet concentrated enough in his bloodstream to chase away the crash. Itaku culture called it the "himitsu hangover." He hid under the comforter with his comm, and let the network flow that he'd avoided during the days when they'd been working the Everett job wash over him. Pings from friends and acquaintances, dull spam from legit organizations, clever spam that snaked through his filters and agents... He skimmed the flow going to his legit identity, then flipped over to his anonymizer and hit the itaku flow. It was the PacAm scene's usual mix of gossip, magical backchannel chatter, and ego trashfires. He was drowsily skimming recent threads on the itaku boards when one of them made him pause.

> Some flash dai'takus screwed their Johnson's pooch last night and put their hoppers through a hornet's nest of magical drek [dicksploit.875935x805k7.stl.nacf.mtx]
>
> -------------
>
> no shit rip vanwinkle. !=nice prox btw [pwnytr0n.273936x758q9.slo.cfs.mtx]
>
> -------------
>
> Th3rdR417 finally stepped on himself n got fried dumbshit had it coming swore id never work w tht frakjob again [gammagurl.947937x825q2.sea.nacf.mtx]
>
> -------------
>
> well not ne mor. that thresh is magical meatpaste nao I guess '~' [hellhound_poo.381938x805q7.van.nacf.mtx]
>
> -------------

HARD CHUMMERS NEED HARD PROTECTION
PROOF UR CACHE W ITAKU MUTUAL
[itakuinsurance4u839939x8012q2.sea.nacf.mtx]

----

frakking spammers
[hellhound_poo.381940x805q7.van.nacf.mtx]

----

sweet gaia RIPing in the burbs 2 can u imagine so amscai
[saltylicrish.6428941x402f9.pdx.cel.mtx]

That was the first time he'd seen a name thrown out in connection with the blast that had triggered the BoeMaru lockdown. He didn't know the dead thresher personally, but he'd heard Th3rdR417 had built a high-wattage reputation among the Johnson class for audacious burglary work. The word within the PacAm itaku scene, however, suggested his work only succeeded because he ran with more cautious teammates who picked up his slack. Some teams could operate successfully that way, but those always had a symbiotic dynamic to balance it out. The oblique sniping from Th3rdR417's anonymous former teammates suggested he hadn't learned how to give as generously as he received. Whit's curiosity sharpened, and he flipped over to the SEAplex commercial news feeds.

Library Explosion Kills at Least Three;
Faulty Gas Main Suspected
Several persons were killed and one injured

Thursday afternoon when an explosion rocked the basement of the Alderwood Library in Snohomish County. The blast is thought to have been caused by a rupture in the building's gas line. The building was mostly empty at the time, as the security system had triggered an evacuation a half-hour before the explosion. Emergency responders were not notified until after the explosion, however, because of a fault in the security system. Two of the deceased have been identified as contract janitorial staff; the other remains have yet to be identified. The surviving casualty is a student at the near-by Edmonds Community College who was working part-time at the library as a security officer. They are in stable but serious condition at Cascade Memorial Hospital.

The Alderwood Library. Its two distinctions were the early twentieth century WPA murals that hung in its foyer, which Whit only knew about because of the library's second distinction: its large collection of Hermetic magical texts. Most of them had been digitized and were freely accessible from the matrix, though. The collection had some rare volumes, but no particularly dangerous or interdicted materials. As far as he had heard, there was nothing there that would cause the kind of damage they'd seen in their astral drive-by, or warrant the kind of protection (or worse, failsafe) that could. The explosion at the library would have seemed like a random accident, if it weren't for the itaku chatter lighting up the boards, and that he had seen the strange aftermath himself.

Contract janitorial staff. Yeah, sure they were. And he was a disaffected printmaker. He called M'pixl-tpff. The spirit materialized with an aggressively cheerful *pop*.

"Hiiiiiiiya, buddy! Whatcha up to?" They zipped around the bedroom, making faces at the goldfish in the bowl on the dresser and opening drawers at random.

"Heya. I've got something for you to check out."

The buzzing of the spirit's pixie wings intensified. They darted in close to Whit's face. "Oooh? Maaaayhem?"

"What? No! We've had this talk. Mayhem is bad for you."

The spirit pouted, and their wings drooped. The buzzing fell in pitch.

"Something happened yesterday at the Alderwood Library. I need you to find how it involved magic. Like, big-time, magical secret-type stuff. And if itakus were there? One of them might have been a guy named Th3rdR417. Who were they, who hired them." Whit waved his hand. "That kind of stuff."

The spirit looked up. "Secret magic?"

"Secret magic or magical secrets. There was an accident, an explosion, I guess, and—"

"MAYHEM!" The spirit clapped their hands in delight, their eyes bright and keen. "Yaaaaaay!"

Whit's shoulders slumped. It occurred to him (not for the first time) that mages in the fifteenth century probably had an easier time applying the advice that Abraham of Worms had left about being a responsible communicant for one's Holy Guardian Angel.

"I'll find out all the secrets!" The spirit cheered and threw their arms in the air as they flew a double loop around his head. "You can count on meeeeee!"

Whit sighed as his spirit popped out of the room. He'd been trying to limit M'pixl-tpff's exposure to negative experiences since that illuminating (and mortifying) discussion about the sympathetic permeability of the HGA/mage relationship he'd had with—he shook his head. No. This would be fine. Honestly, there was a good chance there wasn't anything interesting to find. The other team of itakus was just as likely to have been on a routine job, didn't keep their edge sharp, and got burned thanks to Th3rdR417's notorious sloppiness. M'pixl-tpff would probably get bored and flutter off to the Lynnwood megamall nearby for people-watching, anyway. His own team working a job in Everett at the same time the Alderwood blew sky-high, just as high-wattage itakus were working it, was probably coincidence and nothing more.

That didn't stop his intuition from nagging at him, though. It would be good to know for certain that the library accident was unrelated, just to shut it up.

Three hours later, Whit had migrated from the bedroom to

his apartment's spartan living room. He'd traded the warmth of his comforter for a vicuña sweatshirt that he remodded out of a dirty base layer lying on the floor. He'd stopped doing laundry once the realization hit him in college that magical remodding not only made one garment into a different one in terms of style. It also turned a dirty piece of clothing into a new, *totally clean* one. That had been a revelation. He soon learned that a gulf of practical knowledge and magical practice separated remodding clothes from remodding clothes *well*. He thus stumbled into the mundane mysteries of fiber, cut, and construction. Mastering the magical ability had taken an unexpectedly large amount of hands-on interdisciplinary study, but it was so worth it to never do laundry again.

When M'pixl-tpff reappeared, Whit was still tracking the boards, but had switched his synthcaf to a racetam focus and synthesis blend. The itaku community had released its pent-up resentment towards Th3rdR417 in a flood of snide innuendo and conspiracy theories. These mutated quickly as posters tried to one-up each other, but here and there an enlightening signal would cut through the noise. One of the more verifiable threads pointed to an old mages' forum long since locked and abandoned. It surfaced the credible existence of a warded archive, located secretly and securely several floors below ground at the Alderwood.

M'pixl-tpff's wings beat out a driving staccato upon their return, a good indication that their goal had been fulfilled and then some. Expressions of calculated nonchalance and unabashed eagerness fought on the small spirit's face, the latter winning out when Whit greeted them.

"Ahhhh, soooo many secrets!" they squealed and pressed their hands to their cheeks. "And so much mayyyyhem," they breathed.

Whit groaned and rubbed his forehead. He'd have to figure out a better way to discourage the spirit's unhealthy interest in pandemonium. "Okay, buddy. What's the scoop?"

The spirit paused in mid-air, their brow wrinkled in confusion.

Whit shook his head. "I mean, what did you find out? About the library?"

"There were bad people like you guys, who broke into the library…"

"We're not 'bad people,'" Whit equivocated. "Well, maybe Bob is." He paused to think it over and found himself nodding. "Yeah, Bob is pretty bad. Even if he does seem to like animals. And S2K is kind of an enabler, huh," he muttered. "What were they after?"

"The Alamo doesn't have a basement, but this place sure did!"

"The what? What does that have to do with—"

"Nuh-thing! Because it doesn't have a basement." M'pixl-tpff leaned in. Whit leaned forward, too, in encouragement.

"Especially not a seeecret basement, with wards and barriers and spells and stuff that goes *kablooey* in your faaaace!" The spirit shouted and shook their hands in the air, laughing hysterically.

Whit felt another piece of the puzzle slide into place. "So the warded archive was real. What was in there?"

"A book, old books." The spirit leered. "Naughty books."

"They were paid to go after porn?" He was disappointed that, despite all the wonders of the Immanent world, the client class could be so banal in its habitus.

"Mmmm, nope nope nope." M'pixl-tpff wagged a finger. "*Naughty* books. Books that nice mages shouldn't play with."

"Goetic texts?"

"Booooring." The spirit made a grandiose show of yawning.

He laughed in assent. "Okay, give me a hint."

M'pixl-tpff sang, "Taking the Vespers, gonna make lots of someones take the Big Sleep…"

Whit cocked his head. "Not the *Black Vespers*?"

"Ding-ding-ding!" The spirit tapped the tip of Whit's nose.

"Are you sure?" He looked down with a frown. The *Black Vespers* was one of those footnotes of pre-Immanentization magical history that everyone swore existed but no one had ever seen personally. Macabre stories surrounded the book, no matter that they were probably apocryphal. More reliable accounts describe the text containing rituals to open doors to planes not otherwise accessible by magic from here. Those accounts were conspicuously agnostic about the historical catastrophes purportedly linked to it. He folded his arms and held one elbow in hand as he bit his thumb in thought. "They were after an old magic book, and you're sure that was the title?"

"Yeeeees," said M'pixl-tpff. They mimicked Whit's expression and pose. "Serious business. Gotta get it. Be sure. Our Mr. Johnson was veeeeery particular. Oh yes! Big-time himitsu. No one should be watching. Other things to look at." The spirit blew up its cheeks and pantomimed an explosion, then shook their head with disappointment. "But the air machines didn't blow up, so watching they were! He didn't expect that."

"Who was 'our Mr. Johnson?'"

"Yes." The spirit nodded happily.

"No. I mean, who was their Mr. Johnson."

"*Yes,*" M'pixl-tpff replied in elvish, rather smugly.

"Wait, what?" Whit's gaze snapped back up, and he scowled at the spirit as suspicion bloomed into dismay and in rapid succession fruited into anger. He yelled, "Our Mr. Johnson was *their* Mr. Johnson?"

The spirit steepled their index fingers together and pressed them against their mouth. They looked at Whit with wide eyes and pursed lips.

He took a deep breath and closed his eyes. He silently counted to ten in Enochian, mentally focusing his frustration to a point with each increment. Holding that intention, he counted backwards to one before he released it. Tension drained out of his body, and he could feel his shoulders drop away from his ears like a taut wire had been cut.

Whit opened his eyes and gazed softly at the spirit. "LAIAD

OMAOAS LEL CHIS?" he asked in Enochian, careful to keep his voice even.

The spirit smiled with delight and nodded emphatically. "Yes!" They shot a finger in the air and twirled. "The same the same thaaa saaaaaaaame."

Whit spun away and swore. "DONASDOGAMA," he breathed. "Son of a bitch thought he was using us for max-tac diversion while he bought a milk run at the library."

He spun back to face M'pixl-tpff. "You." He pointed a finger at the spirit. "Go find a holly wreath and take it to the sap who was on security. It's okay to leave it in their room if they're still in the hospital. Or—no. Flowers. Flowers are happier? Bring them an amaryllis. White, no—holy frak! That's morbid. Better make it red. But it's also the solstice. If you can find a yellow clivia instead…"

The spirit stared at him, hanging in mid-air with a slack jaw and a dazed expression. Whit held up his hands.

"Never mind all that. Just find some nice flowers and bring them to the person who was hurt." He smiled, his mouth tight. "There's someone I need to have a conversation with."

M'pixl-tpff gave him a double thumbs-up. "You can count on me, buddy! Anything else? Need help dishing out the what-for?"

Whit was already heading back to the bedroom to shower and remod a suit with appropriately intimidating tailoring. "Oh, I think I've got that covered," he growled. He started building the visualization. Long-staple merino to give the seams sharp precision. Ten percent silk in the worsted yarn, the added luster would make the black appear darker. In a formal barathea weave…

He pulled his sweatshirt over his head and threw it across the floor. No, fuck it. To hell with subtlety. This called for more extreme measures.

Whit stalked up the walkway alone to the deconsecrated church where Alcime Vannetais lived, the wind whipping at the thick crest of his upswept hair. The limestone building had been built at the turn of the twentieth century. It was rezoned as residential space and converted to condos a few years after the turn of the twenty-first. The awkward units distinguished themselves from other luxury developments of the time by their mystifying layouts and nightmarish distributions of space. This gave them architectural credibility, but offered little livability or domestic harmony in return. A suspicious poltergeist haunting in the 2030s was rumored to have been orchestrated by one of the residents in retaliation for noise complaints made by another. It had resulted in such extensive (and disturbing) damage to all twelve units that the building sat empty for over a decade, at which point a shell company had quietly approached the individual owners. It bought them out at a steep discount to market value, and renovated the building once again. The latest renovation retained the original stained glass, exposed masonry, and Neoclassical details that made the property desirable the first time around, but transformed the previous maze of Irrationalist units into seven larger, more serene spaces designed according to San Yuan Feng Shui.

Vannetais owned an apartment in the southeast corner, with a birch tree shading its private entrance. Whit paused at the bronze door and slid into the astral plane to announce himself to the watcher spirit guarding the threshold. There were multiple warded barriers in place. The wards protected the space from intrusion and observation on both the astral and material planes, and made it impossible for him to locate Alcime's aura. The spirit signaled him to wait, then departed through the nearest barrier without a word. The spirit returned almost as soon as it had left. A series of barriers dropped as it bowed and moved aside. Whit left the astral plane and heard a latch slip, and the door in front of him cracked outward. He heaved it all the way open and stomped inside in the direction the spirit indicated.

Whit found the elven mage upstairs in his study, where he sat behind a dark wood desk that faced the open doorway. Vannetais appeared to be engrossed in multiple documents on its smartdisplay top and did not look up when he entered in high dudgeon. A tall, narrow stained glass window was set in the stone wall to his left. It was rotated open on a bearing hinge set in the middle of its top and bottom edges, and the birch tree outside filtered what pale light the overcast day allowed to shine in. The breeze from the open window was gentle and temperate, despite it being the middle of December.

"Ah, Erskine. I was hoping you would drop by. Have a seat." The other mage gestured idly to his right, where two low armchairs sat near a bank of square windows, their glass in the same geometric pattern as the one by the desk.

Whit folded his arms and scowled at the elf, whose head was still down. His blond hair fell loose around his face, catching the sun from the open window. "No." At this, Alcime looked up with a bemused expression that irritated him even more.

"Something troubling you?" he asked mildly. "Was there a problem with the cred transfer?"

"Really, Alcime?" Whit laughed sharply, in disbelief. "The *Black Vespers?*"

The elf shrugged but did not drop his gaze. "Some doors have keys."

"Some doors should stay closed," Whit returned. He cringed inwardly at how his voice sounded, too loud for the room.

"Some doors are already open." Alcime cocked his head. "And ought to be shut."

Whit swallowed involuntarily as a chill prickled his skin. The abstract disapproval he had initially felt turned into a tangible fear, crawling across his scalp and down his neck. "What have you done?" he whispered.

Alcime did look away then. He tilted his head upward and

watched the skeletal shadows of birch branches play upon the ceiling above them.

"Nothing—yet." A ghost of a smile passed over his lips. "Aside from encouraging a minor act of vandalism to distract from an unscheduled visit to the sub-basement of the Alderwood Library." He looked sidelong at Whit.

"Minor vandalism?" Whit's jaw fell open. He welcomed the resurgence of indignation that chased away his dread. "You hired us as a smokescreen while you stole an interdicted book from a public library!"

Alcime laughed. "Don't be ridiculous, Erskine. Of course I didn't."

Whit relaxed a little, and his tight shoulders eased away from his ears.

"I used you as a smokescreen for the team of professional thieves already hired to discretely acquire a rare book from a sequestered collection for me." A dark look briefly broke through the elf's composure. "Under an unfortunately idiosyncratic definition of 'discretion,' as it turned out."

"How could we be the smokescreen? You hired us for the most uneventful—" He caught himself. "Probably one of the most uneventful jobs in the history of the itaku underground."

Alcime tipped his head to the side. "You and your affiliates do possess a certain reputation."

"Because we're so hyper-talented and do amazingly stylish

work?"

"That would be one way to describe the dramatic flavor of casualties, calamity, and general mayhem you seem to leave in your wake, yes."

Whit flinched at Alcime's choice of words. "We *are* itakus. A casual relationship with law and order comes with the job?"

Alcime pursed his lips in thought, then began counting off on long, graceful fingers. "Assassinating a sitting NACF senator—"

Whit interrupted. "The assassination part wasn't us. That was his wife."

"Duly noted." The elf dipped his head with an elegant acknowledgment. He continued his list, ticking off more fingers. "The arson, and subsequent wildfire, that razed an NACF Historic Landmark estate and two hundred acres of nature preserve to the ground. The largest corporate naval explosion on the northern Pacific coast since 2061. The largest radioactive disaster North America has seen in a generation."

"Mount Rainier was not our fault!" Whit started to hold up his own finger in protest, then thought better of it. He ran his hand through his hair, instead, his fingers snagging in the stiff thicket. "Not directly, at least," he mumbled.

Alcime began ticking off fingers on his other hand. "The sabotage, and subsequent sinking, of a flying casino that took hundreds of lives with it on its maiden voyage."

Whit growled at the unhappy memory. "Fucking Milkboy."

"Which in turn inspired a NeuroSim transmedia phenomenon that, as I understand it, has spawned quite a popular fandom with the young people."

"Stop, please." The *Passion Above the Clouds* franchise was a thinly veiled fanfiction written about them by a previous Johnson (to her great commercial success). To learn that Alcime knew about it was … mortifying. Whit groaned and pressed the heels of his palms to his eyes. He stopped after a moment and dropped his hands. "You're the one who hired us, planning on a catastrophic result, so how am I the one who feels like an asshole?"

"Because you still possess a conscience, wayward though it may be, and because I am being emotionally manipulative to prove a point."

Whit met his stare. "I don't understand."

Alcime sighed and broke eye contact. He gazed at the shelves of bound books behind Whit.

"The ignorance with which most people live their lives is an unconscious surrender to the rota fortuna. Things 'just happen' to them. It is easy and blameless to pant beneath its yoke of servitude, compared to the terrible responsibility of the alternative." He shifted his focus and leaned to look out the open window on his left. The late-afternoon glow from the golden stained glass washed over his face. "Acting mindfully, actively engaging with the consequences." He paused. "Self-knowledge can either be the millstone that drowns you, or, harnessed to your will, become the lodestone by which you steer towards enlightenment." He looked back at Whit hopefully.

Whit hadn't expected this response, and he was finding it difficult to maintain the wounded pride that had driven him to confront the elven mage. The adrenaline was draining out of him, and this oddly earnest turn in Alcime caught him off guard and confused him. He stuffed it away to process later when he had a clearer head, and deflected the conversation back to his original grievance. "We really were the JV squad all along."

Alcime's lips slid into a sly smile. "I had thought of you as more the club team, to be honest. But, I have to say, you came out of this ahead."

"Oh, yes. Your outing me by name as an itaku was such a bonus." Whit mustered the energy to glare at the elven mage, who snorted with amusement.

"Hardly. With all the masking you do, all they know is that they may have employed a relative of the presumably late Lambert Erskine on a small project for the greater good of the community."

Whit swallowed reflexively as he felt the familiar wave of panic roll through him at the mention of his father's name. He clenched his fists and continued to glower at the other mage, not trusting himself to speak without making the situation more complicated.

Alcime raised an eyebrow at his anxious response but didn't provoke him further. He searched Whit's face. The laughter in his expression softened, and he made a placatory gesture. "That might have been indiscrete of me. I apologize and hope it presents no inconvenience to you in the future."

Whit felt an involuntary smile try to sneak out. He clenched his jaw and looked away.

"Honestly, you should thank me. The others were very impressed by your performance. It will be good for your, ah, 'street cred.' The Abyssal Nexion and the Fellowship have separately expressed appreciation for the 'booby trap' electrical system that you apparently included in the installation, albeit probably not for the same reasons."

"I'll pass the compliment on to the chef," Whit said distractedly. Their team didn't advertise openly, unlike some of the flash famerunners who actively marketed themselves on the more feral side of the matrix. Still, a little rep boost might not be bad for business. He knew Bob and Sakura would prefer to work more often. Picking up jobs at a roughly bi-monthly rate synced with his flâneur lifestyle, but he still had more than Y200,000 in school loans hanging over his head. He scowled when he considered how much of his itaku earnings had already gone towards paying off the balance.

"Don't play the petulant brat, Erskine. It's unattractive." The elf sighed and closed his eyes. His lips twitched in response to a conversation Whit could not hear. After a moment, a spirit of air materialized in the room. It had the face and upper body of an elderly man, but its lower half was a slowly churning funnel of cloud. It held out a slim octavo bound in viridian calfskin. A monad symbol was embossed in gold on the volume's slightly scuffed front cover.

Whit looked with suspicion at the book. "Is this supposed to ensure my silence? Make me complicit in the theft?"

"No. It's supposed to be a peace offering, to assuage any feelings of ill use." Alcime sounded disappointed. He regarded the tome in the spirit's hands with weariness. "The other itakus brought back several titles as well as the one I had requested. They had hoped it might earn them a bonus, but frankly I suspect the survivors grabbed everything on the shelf without looking when they panicked and left their colleagues to die."

Whit took the book from the spirit and opened it. It was beautifully bound in the old style, he had to admit. The pages were linen paper printed wth ink, not programmable digital leaves. He bit his lip when he saw the frontispiece and recto title. "A private edition of the *Liber Loagaeth*?"

"Not exactly. This is an annotated text with glosses Dee wrote. Translation notes, mostly, with some personal observations, although they never made it into the catalog of his library. Neither Cotton nor Ashmole knew they existed. The original was found stuffed behind chimney bricks in one of the bedrooms in the house at Mortlake. Insulated against hellfire, if one believes the story." He paused. "This is a facsimile, obviously. Rumor says the codex itself is locked in a Swiss vault. Slightly harder to get to than a public library, even a well-warded one."

Whit opened his mouth to speak, then closed it and frowned crookedly.

"Go," Alcime said. He drew out a pair of display goggles and augmentation gloves from one drawer in the desk, and a sheaf of papers from another. Without looking up, he made shooing motions toward Whit and the door. "Go home. Play with your new toy. It's the solstice, and I have work to do."

"Heyyyy, buddy!" M'pixl-tpff appeared in front of Whit and swarmed him as soon as he passed through the unseen astral barrier that barred the spirit access to Vannetais' front door. "What happened? How'd it go? Didja give him the what-for?" The spirit shadowboxed the air with a determined, martial expression on their face.

"Oh, yes. What-for was given, all around." Whit smiled ruefully, but felt better for their optimistic confidence in him. "C'mon. We have a solstice party to get to."

"Yaaaaaay! I love parties! They're almost as much fun as secrets!" M'pixl-tpff flew a few loops, then settled in the air next to him as he walked away from the building.

He pulled up the furry hood of his parka against the cold rain that had begun to fall with slow, fat drops. "I said that I'd bring the eggnog and brandy, and I need to stop by the quick-fab store to pick up that model helicopter print I ordered for Billy's Secret Santa gift."

"A Secret Santa is the best Santa!" The spirit clapped in approval, then sighed morosely. "I didn't find any good secrets. It was boring out here. Oh! How about you? Did you find any?" They pressed their hands to their face, pushing up their cheeks. "Ohhhh, I bet there were sooo many in there."

"A couple." Whit hummed vaguely. He slid his hands into his coat pockets and thought about his meeting with Alcime as he wandered toward the bustle of the Pike/Pine corridor. He slowed as he realized that, by goading him about the other team of itakus and Whit's own insecurities, the other mage had largely sidestepped the matter of the *Black Vespers*. Clever bastard. He didn't like admitting it to himself, but he was more relieved than angry that Alcime hadn't wanted to discuss it. He could, however, freely admit to feeling put out that his brilliantly obnoxious velvet suit hadn't elicited any reaction or comment. He hadn't quite gotten the lightwell effect right on the tonal red-on-red dragon scales, but he had created a plausible rendition of nanomere-attenuated ulfire. A little more practice, and he might win that bet with Sakura. On the other hand, the suit was totally the wrong thing to wear to a Polynesian-themed solstice party. He sighed.

"Hey—about…my coming here. Let's make that a secret!" Whit's voice took on the preternatural cheerfulness that seemed to emerge against his will whenever he had a fraught request to ask M'pixl-tpff.

"Ooookay, you got it, buddy! My lips are sealed! Silent as the—wow!" The spirit materialized fully. They grabbed Whit's sleeve with glee and pointed down the street with their free hand. "Look at the Christmas sweater on that dog!"

Whit felt a pulsing on his wrist, and looked down to see a call waiting on his comm. He recognized Sakura's ID and answered.

"Hey, why are you in Cap Hill? What are you up to?" she asked.

Whit winced. He had forgotten to turn off the comm's custom geo-syncing that the team used during jobs.

"Uh, I was just … out, taking my ontologically suspect angel for a walk," Whit replied after a pause. The book Alcime had given him felt heavy in his coat pocket. "Why?"

"Can you pick up an order for tonight at Glyph Bakery, since you're over there? Their delivery drone brought the wrong order. They don't have another launch open until Monday because of the holiday weekend, and all my drones are busy."

"Is that Sakura?" M'pixl-tpff whipped around on buzzing pixie wings. "Hi, Sakura!!!" the spirit yelled at the comm. "No secrets here!" They flashed him a sharp smile and dematerialized.

Whit sensed the spirit's excitement as they flew across the street toward the dog. "Um, okay," he said, momentarily distracted by M'pixl-tpff 's potent enthusiasm for hideously festive knitwear and mundane animals wearing human clothing. "Yeah, of course."

"Thanks a bunch! The order's under Machen. See you at the lodge."

She signed off, and the comm went silent. Whit stared at it for moment, irresolute, then called her back.

"Problem with the bakery?"

"No, I'm still on my way over. It's just that..." He paused to collect his thoughts. "That blast yesterday? Th3rdR417 was one of the itakus who RIPed out on it."

"Seriously?" She chortled. "It's about time. I've met the guy. He's an idiot."

"Really?"

"Really he's an idiot, or really did I meet him?"

"The latter. I mean, the former is common knowledge."

"Oh, yeah. It was at one of Roni's parties. He kept trying to tell everyone that *Passion Above the Clouds* was based on *his* adventures as an itaku."

"What the frak?"

"Right? This is what you miss when you ghost on her invites."

"I know, I know. I just get the feeling that I'm invited to be there on display, like a trophy or something."

"Yeah, well, then she invites these other jokers to take your place."

"Th3rdR417 wasn't even a mage!"

"No, but he was a thresher, which for mundanes is basically the same thing. And he was really charismatic, too. Had style. Minimal body fat. I can see why Roni invited him. Good party material. I should've scanned him for modeling, when I had the chance."

Whit snorted and rolled his eyes. "Well, he's dead now." He reoriented himself and began walking toward Glyph, following his comm's haptic cues. "Plus, I doubt you could afford to license him for shoots, even if he weren't."

"Careful, or someone might get the wrong idea that you're jealous of a dead man," she sang. "But yeah, Th3rdR417 didn't come cheap." She tutted, but he couldn't tell if it were in admiration or distain. "I hope the Johnson didn't pay them in advance for that job."

Whit froze. "I know who hired them."

"Some slot who didn't do their homework before hiring their team, obvs. Who cares?"

"No, that's not—"

"Look, we'll talk about it later if you want. Okay? Now go get our grub, or we'll be stuck consecrating our winter solstice ritual with nothing but this random birthday cake they mis-delivered and the expired soynuts Billy keeps in the lodge kitchenette for emergencies."

He laughed, both at the absurdity and his friend's utter indifference to itaku intrigue, and it was a welcome release that chased away his pensive ruminations. He could brood about Alcime and whatever their exchange had meant later. Tonight they witnessed the end of one year and the dawn of another, metaphorically at least, for the lodge and their fellowship.

"On my way."

He closed the connection. He sensed M'pixl-tpff watching him with indecision, and the spirit's desire to follow the dog unseen pulled at him. He let them go, with a wave and a small smile. Whit slid his hands back in his coat pockets and strolled down the street, as the streetlights above him bloomed in the darkening twilight.

A Boon for Baphomet

ACKNOWLEDGMENTS

THANKS FOR READING *A Boon for Baphomet*. I hope you had as much fun with it as I had writing it. A host of people helped make this book happen.

First, it's all Tony Scaletta's fault for making that fateful joke tweet on a December morning in what feels like an aeon ago (really, just 2015). *A Boon for Baphomet* started out as a short farce in response to those 132 characters, but the muse, having other ideas, took that story between her teeth and ran with it like a *mari lwyd* hobby horse on fire.

My beta readers generously gave needed feedback and engagement from the beginning—thank you all!

The developmental notes Stephen Conway provided on an earlier version of the manuscript were thoughtful, kind, and terrifically useful.

Thanks also go to Cameron Harris for editing an early version of the manuscript. (If you find any typos or crimes committed against the English language, worthy readers, be assured that they're my fault alone.)

And my deepest gratitude to my lovely and talented spouse,

whose support of this endeavor (and me) has been enthusiastic and unflagging, even on days when mine wasn't.

ZORGE, y'all.

About the Author

DeWitt Wilcox (twitter: @maniraptor) lives in Athens, Georgia, to the befuddlement of everyone, and still hasn't gotten used to the fact that the dirt there looks like it came from Mars.

FURTHER READING

IF YOU'D LIKE TO READ more from the Itaku Underground, why not join the Itaku update list?

What you'll get:

• ITAKU SUPPLEMENTAL #01, a free supplemental codex with author's notes on magic, Enochian translations, and more. (It's like the director's commentary but, you know—for books!)

• a heads-up on new Itaku books, free shorts and supplementals, and giveaways.

New updates generally go out once every quarter. (A little more often if there is a launch coming up. A little less often if I'm hip-deep in work and have forgotten what ~~month week~~ day it is.) I'll never share or sell your email or information, and you can unsubscribe anytime.

Sign up at: **http://eepurl.com/cNa5J1**

www.ingramcontent.com/pod-product-compliance
Lightning Source LLC
Chambersburg PA
CBHW021016120726
47905CB00009B/3034